COME INSIDE
A DARK WHY CHOOSE ROMANCE
SAGE RELLEANNE

Rainbow Publishing House LLC

Copyright © 2024 by Sage RelleAnne

CONTENTS

Introduction	V
	VII
Dedication	VIII
Playlist	IX
Prologue	1
1. Yara	2
2. Yara	8
3. Kazi	15
4. Yara	21
5. Mateo	23
6. Yara	24
7. Mateo	31
8. D	33
9. Mateo	34
10. Kazi	38
11. Yara	42
12. Yara	46
13. J.W.	51

14.	Yara	56
15.	Yara	60
16.	D	63
17.	Yara	65
18.	Mateo	74
19.	J.W.	76
20.	Yara	79
21.	Mateo	86
22.	Yara	88
23.	J.W.	92
24.	Kazi	94
25.	Yara	98
26.	D	100
27.	Yara	101
28.	Kazi	111
29.	Yara	118
30.	J.W.	124
31.	Mateo	127
32.	Yara	129
33.	Yara	131
Epilogue		139
About the author		144
Sneak Peek		145

INTRODUCTION

Hi y'all,

This has gone through several rounds of editing and a round of proof-reading. If anything still managed to slip through, please let me know. My email is sagerelleanne@gmail.com.

If you have not read anything by me yet, a few things before you buckle into this wild ride.

I write in both first and third person. This will be pretty consistent among all of my novels. For this one Yara is in first POV and the men will be in third.

Most have loved this, but some have **not**.

Now that, that's out of the way, thank you so very kindly for giving my book a read. I greatly appreciate your support!

Okay I promise that's everything (besides the triggers).

VERY IMPORTANT

This book has quite a few trigger warnings.

For an extensive in-depth list please reach out to me at: sagerelleanne@gmail.com

Brief outline of the main triggers:

Heavy self-deprecation

BDD

Mentions of childhood abuse (not graphic or in detail)

Mentions of domestic violence (including SA, not graphic or in detail)

Blood & Gore

Murder

Stalking

BC Tampering

This book was made possible by all my lovely readers.
Be it beta, ARC, or those that found me in other ways.
Your support and love of Izzy's story paved the way to Yara's.
I will say... hers is quite a bit darker.

DEDICATION

This one is for all you beautiful people that can't look into a mirror without finding a flaw.
You are not alone.
You are worthy.
You are perfect just the way you are.
Ignore the voices saying otherwise.
Even your own.

PLAYLIST

While writing this book I listened to this playlist on repeat.

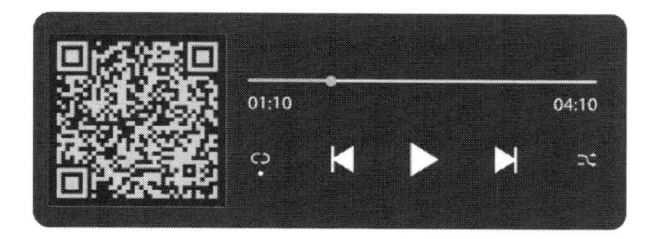

PROLOGUE

Yara stepped under the shower's hot mist. She wasn't sure if this was a mistake or not. She let out a shuddering breath and dug her nails into her legs to steady her racing heart.

Yara was anxious. Nervous. *Excited*.

The flurry of emotions were caused by her plans.

They were simple.

By the end of the night, Yara would be filled with cum by a man twice her age.

Chapter 1

YARA

I had been told my entire life that I was beautiful, a perfect angel, sexy personified. For a while I believed it, even after everything I was put through, but then every time I looked in the mirror, I would find something I didn't like.

My uneven knees, my stomach that would never flatten, the fat on my cheeks.

A new scar. A purple bruise. A broken bone.

The more compliments that were bestowed onto me, the more I hated myself. The more I believed I would never live up to the expectations.

The more my mind rebelled.

Until a particularly awful experience back home left me a broken mess.

I could no longer ignore the scars—the *deformities*—that covered my body. A testament to my childhood.

Now my mirrors stayed covered, and I hid myself in loose dark clothes. Away from the world's watchful eye. Away from men's leering stares. Away from my own gaze.

Because no matter what I did or how I changed... No matter how much I dieted or exercised...

I would never be beautiful. I was ugly. Inside and out.

Pressure on my temple jostled me out of my spiraling.

"Miss Yara, you had that look on your face again. What are you thinking about?" Of course it was my *assistant*.

"Kazi, I told you to just call me Yara. We have known each other for almost ten years now." I smiled fondly at the man, taking him in. At least he wasn't calling me Miss Greene anymore–that *only* took a year or two to fully break.

Kazi wasn't particularly large or bulky but that was something I loved the most about him. I felt comfortable with him in my orbit. It was hard to describe Kazi, but I would call him pretty. Full lips, sharp angles, flecked russet eyes. Dark ebon hair that fell just over his ears, covering them. He was older than me, but he didn't have a single wrinkle to show for it.

I was jealous.

He leaned down over the chair I sat in until his lips were just a few inches from mine. I stiffened.

"Miss Yara, I wouldn't dream of it. Now come on, we have a full day planned." His dark eyes paused on my mouth, his lips twisted into a grin before he pulled back and swiftly spun my chair away until I was facing my desk.

I refocused on my computer. The black screen's reflection is what originally pulled me into my thoughts of unwanted self-deprecation. I quickly shut my eyes after hitting the power button, only able to catch just the brief outline of my hair.

The blonde was an unruly fluffy mess, and I really ought to cut it all off.

"Miss Yara." Kazi's tone was edged in warning. "The calendar."

I opened my eyes and found the screen was now lit up. I navigated to the schedule for today.

We were fully booked. Again.

"I need to have the one-on-one with Liam, he has already been vetted, but his appointment is tonight, and he requested the discreet package." Most of our clients would meet here in our office, but occasionally, due to the nature of our business, I would need to meet the clients out in the wild.

This one chose a high-end hotel restaurant.

"Not without backup." Kazi stepped up next to me leaning against my desk chair.

I eyed him in my peripheral vision.

He had been extra protective over me since I gained a stalker. I hadn't told Kazi, but I could guess who the threatening letters had been coming from. And it wasn't anybody new.

Men thought that because I ran a dating service, it meant they could treat me how they pleased. They thought I was a sexual deviant waiting to be fucked. It's why I hadn't dated seriously since high school, just a fling here and there to let off some steam. I used a different last name for business purposes, but that didn't mean much when my face had landed on the front page of a few magazines and articles. The popularity of my company was a decidedly double-edged sword.

Even so, I had zero regrets about my company; my only regret was my choice in men. Something I had in common with my bestie, Izzy.

Speaking of...

"I need to call Izzy, she's been having issues with her current trash of the month, Harry."

Kazi sighed exasperatedly. "That woman is ridiculous, it makes sense you two are friends."

"Yeah, so why are you and I friends?" I laughed pushing my shoulder into his side.

"Good point, though you do also pay me." Kazi finally relaxed, leaning further into me and chuckling a bit.

I could feel the heat of his skin even through the suit he currently wore, but I tried my best to ignore it and my body's response to him.

It was getting more and more difficult. At some point I would have to acknowledge my growing feelings. But not today. "Hardee har har. You and I both know you wormed your way into my life on your own. I just offered you money after the fact."

It was true, Kazi was one of the first people I befriended when I ran from my hometown and made the trek out to California. He had always been kind, soft, non-threatening. Others may think that boring and not be interested. But to me? It had the opposite effect.

I thought I would fit in here easily after growing up in Florida. I could not have been more wrong.

But that was okay, I had a company to start up and didn't have much time for fun. In fact, the only time I did enjoy myself was at a local comedy club which was where I met Kazi.

Kazi bent over until his breath was in my ear. "I'll go set up for our next appointment. You aren't meeting Liam alone tonight. You know the rules."

"Fine." I knew Kazi wouldn't take no for an answer. Persistent as fuck, it was why he was in my life at all. I didn't make new friends. Izzy was all I needed; she was the rock that kept me together. Even if she was hundreds of miles away in New York.

He offered me one more warning look, his eyes narrowing, mouth flattening into a line, before exiting my office, shutting the door behind him.

Minimizing the schedule on my computer, I moved to new applications in our main database that hadn't been processed yet. My company, *Darkest Desires,* was in its peak and we had a surplus of applicants everyday. I usually didn't even look through them until their background checks were completed by my team of investigators, but I needed something to focus on.

I scrolled through the pictures before stuttering to a stop, my finger hovering in midair above the mouse.

Striking sage green eyes stared back at me, but that's not what caused me to pause.

I found myself *attracted* to the man in the photo. I could count on two hands the people I had been drawn to in my life. I lifted my finger up in a haze, tracing the outline of the man's sharp jaw, a thin salt and pepper beard covering it. I moved up his face to his shaggy hair that was cropped shorter on the sides and styled on top. It was burgundy with unmistakable grays throughout.

I'm not sure what caused me to peruse further. Perhaps the need for a distraction from Kazi? Maybe the desperate need to pull my mind away from my stalker?

I clicked on his profile.

Forty-six, lived nearby, interested in trying several kinks.

One specifically stood out to me.

Breeding.

My belly pulsated with unexpected desire. A primal urge was riding me. The thought of being filled with cum swirled into my mind, and I rubbed my thighs together in response.

This is new.

As was the interest in a much older man.

Perhaps my daddy issues are finally taking center stage.

Smothering my chaotic thoughts, I read further. He was single, had a vasectomy, and was interested in someone close to his age.

Close to his age.

I certainly wasn't that.

Disappointment coursed through me, immediately followed by surprise.

Was I actually considering using my own dating site? I had started the company on a want to bring light on an otherwise shunned subject.

Venturing into kinks, the taboo, all done in a safe environment. But I had never actually participated.

"You coming?" Kazi poked his head through the door eyeing me speculatively.

I was so lost in thought that I nearly jumped out of my seat. "Yes, one minute."

He raised an eyebrow inquisitively but let me be, shutting the door behind him.

My attention refocused on my computer, and before I could change my mind, I moved the man's profile out of the shared drive and into my personal one, a plan forming in my mind.

I would be reaching out to this man myself.

Chapter 2

YARA

After a long day of nonstop meetings, I was finally back in my office.

"Izzy, come on. You need to visit me before our stupid as fuck reunion in two months, I haven't seen you in too flipping long." Time had slipped by and I was currently changing into my outfit for the dinner with Liam tonight, my phone cradled against my ear. "I miss you and we need to catch up."

"I *know*," Izzy dragged the word out, her voice pitched with emotion even through the phone. "I just... ugh. I don't know what's going on with Harry. He's been acting extra shady and I know he's fucking up, but I need the proof. You know? So he can't fucking lie to me."

I readjusted, quickly tugging my dress over my head as my office door opened. I went to yell at the intruder, but it was just Kazi.

I gestured for him to shut the door. He obliged before leaning back against it. Sometimes I think he forgot he was my assistant, not my personal guard.

"Well, we can agree Harry isn't shit. Did you want me to have Emil look into him?" I asked. Emil was the head of my investigation team for *Darkest Desires*; if there was dirt, I trusted Emil to find it.

Izzy's boyfriend, Harry, didn't seem like a good guy when they met, but you can't tell a woman who to date, they needed to figure it out for themselves.

I knew all about not listening to outside advice.

Izzy was the reason I was brave enough to skip town. She was always there when I needed her. Especially after my break up back home with Daniel.

Now it was time for me to return the favor.

"No, it's okay. I'm going to ask Oliver," Izzy huffed out.

Uneasiness swam in my gut. Shortly after I met Izzy in high school, Oliver started showing up. He was always around, lingering in the background, *watching* her. It was creepy, and she was oblivious. Their friendship had never been healthy, but again, she wouldn't listen to me on any of it.

"Okay..." I finally agreed, unsurely.

"I know, I know. We're too close, blah blah blah. On that front, any news on *your* love life? At this point, I always thought you would be the one married with kids," Izzy joked.

I thought so, too. My mind flipped back to the man on my database before my fingers moved on their own to a scar along my forehead. It had been left by the man I thought would be the father of my children one day.

The man that had kept me from wanting to start a family.

The scar was one of many I had, just another imperfection. I was littered with them.

I could feel Kazi's intense gaze on me as I brushed over the puckered skin, but he had long since stopped asking where it came from. Where any of the scars originated. I gave a different answer every time.

Because the truth?

Well, I hadn't admitted that out loud to anyone besides my therapist.

I wanted to tell Kazi, and I knew I would one day, but not yet.

"Funny. You know I'm too busy being a boss ass bitch. Just like you are." I steered the conversation to safer waters, swallowing down the bile that had made its way up my throat.

I was incredibly proud of Izzy. Her company had grown exponentially over the last few years, and she worked her ass off for it.

The image of the older man from my database flashed into my mind again. This time it was specifically his sage green eyes. Besides my instant attraction to him, there was something about the color that had thrown me off.

They were unsettlingly familiar.

In fact, they looked exactly like Izzy's.

"Random question, you don't have any relatives in California, do you?"

Izzy went uncharacteristically quiet for a moment. "Not anymore," she eventually whispered. "Well hey, I got to go. Love you girl." Her voice took on a fake cheery tone.

Odd.

But I could understand not wanting to talk about family. Izzy and I were close, I would trust her with my life, but even she didn't know the darkness that shrouded my childhood.

And on the flip side of that, I had never even met her mom or step-father.

Izzy never wanted me to come over to her house back in high-school, and I didn't press the matter.

"Love you. Talk soon." Dropping the phone onto my desk, I bent down to slip on my heels. I hated them, but this client had provided my outfit for the evening. All a part of the discretion package.

I attempted to put one shoe on but lost my balance. Before I could fall, strong hands were there to catch me.

"Here, let me." Kazi gently guided me to the velvet couch in my office, pushing me down softly. He turned back grabbing my heels before kneeling in front of me. He had done this before, but watching him in this moment caused my heart to beat rapidly.

Now that I had plans to delve into my own desires, I had opened my mind up to other thoughts. Specifically my interest in Kazi. I had always been drawn to Kazi but never wanted to cross that line. I wouldn't ruin our decade-long friendship over my infatuations.

No matter how strong they were becoming.

Kazi tapped my left foot, and I lifted it up for him. He carefully secured the heel in place, tightening the strap, his fingers leaving a trail of scorching fire. He gently placed my foot onto the ground before repeating the actions with my right.

This time, he didn't let go immediately. Instead, his long gentle fingers wrapped around my ankle, covering the scars there. Another flaw. He looked up, concerned eyes meeting mine. "You haven't been eating again."

I turned my head away in shame. He knew more about me than any other living being, including Izzy. He left me reeling and feeling more vulnerable than I cared to admit.

"I have been, I'm just trying a new diet." The lie clouded the space between us.

His grip on my ankle tightened, causing me to wince in pain. He dropped his hold on it suddenly, standing. Offering me a hand, he carefully lifted me up. Even with the heels on, he still had a few inches on me. However, we were now much closer in height, it made it easier to watch his face as he spoke. "I can't join you tonight, but my cousin is in town and he works in security. He will be there if anything happens." His gaze hopped around the room as he refused to meet my eyes.

Kazi was being uncharacteristically shifty, but I decided not to push it. We were all allowed our secrets.

"Kazi, you know I don't need protection. And even more so, I hate strange men watching me. Just let me go on my own. I'll be at a public restaurant, it's perfectly safe."

"Another letter came in, but I know it won't stop you from your plans tonight." His lips curled up, but his annoyance was palpable. He let me go to grab a folded envelope out of his back pocket. It was already open.

They were always signed the same. The letter D. I could guess who they were from, but I didn't have any proof. Even if I did, I wasn't sure I would tell Kazi my suspicions.

"I told you to stop reading these. They are empty threats. They're from some asshole that doesn't like my company, and you're right, I'm not going to let this *stranger* dictate how I live my life." I was no longer that little girl crying out in fear or that teenager who didn't know any better.

I was nearing thirty years old and I wasn't going to let another man's cruelty affect my life.

Not again.

"If it was nothing to worry about, you would have talked to Izzy about it. You only keep the concerning things from her." He raised an eyebrow in challenge.

I didn't bother arguing. He was right, but it didn't change anything. I may be terrified of eventually coming face-to-face with this stalker, but I was doing my best to not allow it to affect me.

I reached for the envelope, but he held onto it.

"Let me read it."

"What good will that do?" He snatched it back, returning it to his pocket. "The sentiment was the same as all the others."

Which meant a slew of insults calling me every disgusting name under the sun while simultaneously confessing their undying love. I knew the person writing the letters was escalating, but the police didn't care; they practically spewed that I deserved it due to my line of work. As if owning a dating service justified any and all unwelcome advances.

It was certified bullshit.

When I tried to push the issue, showing the authorities a folder of letters and pictures going back *years*, they pointed out that, so far, nothing had actually happened so they weren't threats *exactly*. I couldn't prove I was being followed, the only evidence being the prickle of goosebumps whenever I was out.

Useless. They would only come once a crime was committed, but at that point, it would be too late.

I shut down that line of thinking, containing the full body shiver that threatened to take hold.

The one blessing was that the letters only appeared at the office. They hadn't made their way to my home... yet. But I knew it was only a matter of time. It would only take one slip up.

"Where are you going to be tonight?" I picked up my phone, shoving it into my dress's pocket, the only redeeming feature of this entire ridiculous outfit.

Kazi stayed silent as he took me all in, his full lips now curved distinctly downward into a frown. "I wish you wouldn't let them pick out your clothes. It's bad enough you meet them on these fake *dates*."

I folded my arms across my chest in exasperation. Kazi's dark eyes tracked the motion, but he remained silent.

I didn't want to rehash this argument. Our clients were all thoroughly vetted and these "dates" took place in public establishments. I required all potential clients to have one in-person meeting prior to being matched because background checks didn't exactly work to weed out the assholes. I wanted to ensure all parties that used my services were as protected as I could possibly manage prior to any *activities* occurring. Thus far, we hadn't run into any issues or complaints, and I planned on keeping it that way.

But if the new clients didn't want to be seen at my office? That was where the discretion package came into play.

Additionally, if the initial meeting went sideways, I had learned enough self-defense to take care of myself. "Fine, don't answer my question of where *you're* going to be tonight. I need to get going anyways. Tell your cousin to leave me be, unless he's needed."

Kazi hummed his agreement, leaning forward, close enough that for a moment, I thought he might just kiss me.

My eyes shut on their own accord in anticipation, but instead, I felt as his sturdy hand cupped my cheek softly. My attention found his, he was staring at me with a dark critical intensity, his brow furrowed in concentration.

"Car is waiting for you." His fingers flexed, the rough digits pushing into my skin.

I leaned further into his touch. It snapped him out of whatever trance he was in, causing him to drop his hold and jump back as if I had shocked him.

I didn't say anything. *I couldn't.* I walked swiftly from my office, leaving Kazi behind, attempting to control my breathing and the static that was shooting across my skin in anticipation. Kazi wasn't someone I should ever cross the line with, he was the only constant I had in this city. I needed him, no matter what.

At least that's what I kept telling myself.

I felt his gaze as I made my way to the elevator. Sure enough, when I stepped into it and turned around, he was still standing in my office doorway. His penetrating eyes watched me. It did nothing to quell the building desire that churned in my belly.

I felt as my resolve wavered, but then the elevator doors closed.

I stamped down the feeling and shut my eyes to avoid my reflection.

Chapter 3

KAZI

Kazi pulled out his cell phone and made a call. "It's escalating. He's going to do something worse soon."

"Look, I sent you there to watch over her ten years ago. Do your job."

Kazi growled into the phone, "No, you sent me here to get intel on Izzy. You let me stay when you realized how close they still are. Don't be an ass, Emilio. Or is it Emil now? Don't you think infiltrating her investigative team was a bit overkill?"

"I don't know Kazi, I didn't realize you would take my directive to watch over her so literally. You weren't supposed to become her friend, let alone her assistant, you moronic man."

Kazi didn't bother to correct Emilio. He wanted to be *more* than Yara's friend, but it didn't take much to notice how broken the poor woman was. He was giving her the time she needed to heal. Except after a decade of time he was beginning to suspect she needed more. Another push to make her realize the spectacular woman she was and that he wouldn't be going anywhere. The problem was Kazi recognized abuse victims, and it didn't take long for him to realize her trauma was deeper than she let on.

On the surface, Yara was a beautiful angelic woman, but that wasn't her true self. She was a dark fallen angel; a damaged woman littered with scars both physically and mentally. It made Kazi want her all the more. To protect her. To keep her by his side. To not let the world take another spark of light from her eyes.

Ten years ago, he was livid when he had first been sent out here by his boss, Emilio. He wanted nothing more than to return to the *family* as soon as he could. But not any longer. Now he dreaded the day Emilio tried to drag him home.

Kazi wasn't sure what he would do. He couldn't leave Yara behind.

But could he convince her to join him?

Distracting himself from the depressing line of thought, Kazi looked around the office space. The rest of the employees had long since gone home for the night, and he had business to attend to. Yara wouldn't tell him who she thought the stalker was, but he knew where to look.

"Cat got your tongue? Or are you daydreaming again about a certain blonde haired woman?" Emilio chuckled caustically.

Kazi walked inside Yara's office, shutting the door behind him. "She needed a friend here." He didn't dare lose his temper on Emilio even if he wanted nothing more than to do so in this moment.

"Sure, is that why you wouldn't swap with Mateo? He's interested to see what has kept you in California so long. So fascinated, in fact, he decided to make the trip himself."

Icy dread spread across Kazi's nerves. "You said you were sending Logan."

"Logan is busy handling a different matter. Mateo won't hurt her, he's just curious. From what I heard he's already at the restaurant waiting to be her white knight as needed." Emilio tsked in his ear.

"Fuck, you idiot!" Kazi exclaimed before he could stop himself. "You know how he can be. What happens if he is *interested* in her?" Kazi's heart pounded in his chest, but it was too late now.

"You don't have to worry about that, he never cares about women." Emilio's words did nothing to comfort Kazi and his tone had turned sour.

Kazi knew better than to push him on it.

Emilio and Kazi came from the same *family*, and Mateo was part of it too. In fact he was an integral part–the muscle, the enforcer. He was the boogeyman you never saw coming.

Mateo was uncomfortable, *off*. Kazi hated being in the same vicinity as him, but Mateo wouldn't hurt Yara.

Unless directed to.

Kazi hadn't been part of the *family* very long before Emilio was shipping him off to California with his mission to watch over Yara. Now their only communication was via phone calls and the occasional visit, but even still, Kazi had enough run-ins with Mateo to want to avoid the man.

Refocusing on the task at hand, Kazi entered the password to get onto her computer, but it pinged that it was wrong.

What the fuck?

"She changed her computer password, can you get me the new one?"

Emilio sighed in his ear, annoyed. "Give me a few days. Do you need anything else?"

"Book Mateo a return flight, he can't stay here," Kazi grumbled searching her desk instead.

"You do remember I'm the boss right?" Emilio voiced in warning, he was clearly done with this conversation. "But fine, I'll see what I can do." The phone clicked in Kazi's ear as the call ended.

Kazi was aggravated but used to Emilio's jackass ways. Continuing his search, he combed through Yara's desk and paused as he flipped through the folders on it. Buried in the middle was a large envelope he hadn't seen before, addressed to the deputy that hadn't done much of anything with their concerns.

He opened it, upending its contents.

For a moment, his anger clouded his eyesight, stars shooting across his vision. He blinked a few times. The rage was replaced with disgust; it settled into his gut, an unwelcome guest.

"A fucking *sasaeng*," he muttered under his breath. *An obsessive fan, a stalker.*

There were dozens of pictures of Yara in different locations. Looking through them, he recognized that these pictures spanned several years. Moving the photos aside he found a letter on the bottom.

I will never forget our
time together. Even as
you try to cover it, you
will always wear my
scars.
Only Yours,
-D

Panic slithered up Kazi's throat and he attempted to gulp it down, spluttering out a cough as it choked him. He thought that the stalker was someone new. A random creep that found her from *Darkest Desires*, but he discerned now it was someone else entirely.

This stalker? This person that had been leaving letters? Taking pictures? Attempting to upend Yara's life?

It wasn't a stranger as she had made it out to be.

It was a person from her past.

Someone that she knew.

Kazi heaved a sigh. He had hoped she would trust him with all of her secrets, but he couldn't fault the woman. He wasn't exactly being fully honest with her either.

Kazi replaced the items into the envelope and stuffed it back where he found it.

He decided it was best to *not* leave her with Mateo any longer.

Chapter 4

YARA

This dinner date was in the top three worst I had gone on of all time.

"Yes Liam, but can we please circle back to what you are looking for from my business?"

The table we sat at was in the center of a crowded restaurant. The food looked good, but I hadn't taken more than a few bites, and each one tasted worse than the last.

"Like I said"–smack, smack–"I want a hot blonde, blue eyes, willing to fuck in a hotel after dinner." Liam didn't even look up as he chewed his food with an open mouth.

It took a moment for his words to register.

Not again.

Occasionally clients would ask for the discretion package to try to make a pass at me.

It never worked, other than to frustrate the fuck out of me.

Like in this exact moment. "Will you excuse me? I'll be right back."

Again, he didn't look up from his food, just shooed me away with his free hand.

Now to see if this man was malicious or simply an asshole.

I walked until I was just around the corner where the bathrooms were and then out of sight, I watched Liam.

After a moment he stopped eating and glanced around suspiciously, his hand moving over my drink.

From this distance it was hard to tell if he actually did anything, but I wouldn't be taking my chances. Still hidden around the corner, I flagged our waitress.

"Hi, here's money for the meal and your tip. If you could please be careful when removing my drink, make sure it is dumped. The man should hopefully just leave, but if you have any issues here's my card." I shoved a few hundred at the waitress.

I didn't wait for an answer; I would deal with Liam later.

Right now, I needed a drink.

Preferably one that didn't have the possibility of being laced.

In my haste to leave, I didn't notice that I had left my phone behind.

Chapter 5

MATEO

Mateo was torn. Did he want to wait for the man to finish eating and take the trash out or did he follow the mesmerizing woman that was making her escape out the front door, ducking down as she went. Her small stature made it much easier for her to sneak out.

Technically, Mateo's directive was to watch over her while she was at this dinner.

Mateo twisted back to the man who was now looking around in confusion.

Mateo memorized his face.

He could always finish this business later.

He stood up from his seat in the corner, stretching as he went and cracking his neck. He never underestimated the importance of stretching. Especially at his age.

Mateo threw some money on the table, and after his body was properly adjusted, he made his way to the exit.

Chapter 6

YARA

"Another shot please." This wasn't my typical bar, but it would do. It was lit in red, the drinks were heavy, and it hadn't gotten too busy yet.

I smiled at the bartender as he set my glass down and made my way back to the corner booth. I had zero interest in being social, I wanted to numb some of the aching pain that was threatening to overwhelm me.

I had just enough time to throw back my shot before two men slid into my booth, wedging me in the middle.

If I was a bit more sober, the panic might very well have set in, but I wasn't.

"May I help you?" I asked, not looking at either of them.

"What's a pretty little thing like you doing alone here?" The one to the right leaned in, pressing into my shoulder.

"Waiting for my boyfriend," I stated nonchalantly, adding a shrug for good measure.

"Oh, is that right? You've been waiting for quite some time," The other man advised.

His words sent a chill of unease down my spine.

Exactly how long had they been watching me for?

Across the room, I watched a large barrel chested man I had been keeping tabs on get up. I suspected he was Kazi's "cousin."

"Here he comes now. Sugar!" I waved my hand as the burly man approached.

He looked absolutely nothing like Kazi, but I supposed cousins could do that. Where Kazi was pretty, this man was rugged. Dangerous. He stood well over six feet tall, muscular, and had a shaved beard covering his jaw.

A jolt of desire shot straight to my core as he walked up.

What the fuck?

"Yara," the newcomer stated, his voice gruff from disuse. Calling me by my name confirmed what I already knew–he was the man Kazi sent in his absence. He turned to my unwanted guests; they were no longer arguing with me, instead their faces had turned white.

Men never quite listened when a woman said no. They had to wait for a man to back her up.

One left right away, putting his hands up in surrender, but the other clearly had a death wish.

"I watched you get up from across the room, I bet you her name isn't even Yara. Fuck off man, I found her first."

My hand came up on its own accord, my palm landing up and against the intruder's nose with a satisfying crack.

"You bitch!" He went to raise his hand as if to hit me back, but Kazi's cousin was already there to forcibly remove him.

"I suggest you leave. Now." The voice left no room for argument and this time the sod left without a backwards glance cursing up a storm.

"Sit with me?" I gestured to the now empty spots.

The man furrowed his brow before shrugging. "Might as well. You're not going to ask how I know your name?"

He was surprisingly graceful as he folded himself into the seat, he even kept a respectful amount of space between us.

Which I found unexpectedly annoying.

"Kazi told me his cousin would be keeping an eye on me tonight."

"Did he now? Name's Mateo." He offered me a ginormous hand to shake.

I turned in the booth, giving him mine. It was almost comical the size difference. He gave it a light squeeze before wrapping his thick calloused fingers around my wrist.

"You're ridiculously tiny."

"Uh, thanks?" That was a new one. "How about this? I'm going to get us some shots." I pulled my wrist from his grip and I could see the shock written across his face as I slid out the other side of the booth.

I ordered three shots from the bartender, chugging one before grabbing the other two.

I wasn't exactly thinking straight and Mateo was making it even more challenging. His critical mahogany eyes were following my every move and his attention was causing sparks of anticipation to skitter across my skin.

I wanted to climb this man.

Which was decidedly not a good idea.

My alcohol muddled brain didn't agree.

"Here you go." I didn't return to my seat. Instead, I gave in to my intrusive thoughts. Moving to his side, I settled lackadaisically on his knee that was halfway out of the booth. He stiffened and I attempted to shift and rethink my bold move, but he wrapped an arm around me, securing me in place.

"You're playing a very dangerous game, little bee." His guttural voice was directly in my ear and it sent chills of anticipation to the neediness furling in my belly. One of his arms stayed wrapped around my stomach pressing me against him while the other grabbed his shot. I expected him to drink it, but instead he brought it up to my lips.

"Drink." His voice vibrated against my back. I didn't think to argue, I simply opened my mouth as he pushed the glass against my lips, tipping it up.

I swallowed it down. "Little bee?" I questioned.

"Bright." He set the empty glass on the table. "Lively." He brought his fingers back up to my lips wiping away the burn. "Fierce." He pushed his fingers into my mouth. "Suck on these, show me what you can do before I pull my dick out here and now and fuck you at this table." He readjusted me in his lap until my ass rubbed against his hardened cock.

I hissed at the contact. This wasn't how I thought the night would go, but this beast of a man wasn't putting me on edge as many men before him had.

In fact. It was quite the opposite.

My heart pounding in my chest was from excitement—not the typical fear—as I leaned back further into his embrace.

Is it because he's related to Kazi? Is that why he isn't prickling my anxiety? Why I feel so secure in his arms?

Even though they looked nothing alike.

I sucked down his fingers greedily, swirling my tongue around them. My hand reached down, finding his hard cock, and I brushed along its length through his constricting jeans.

This might not be the smartest idea, but I needed a release. It had been too long. I needed to expel some of my pent up rage, and this man was offering it up to me.

He groaned, removing his fingers, and thrusting upwards into my hand. "Fuck," he expelled, nipping at my ear. "Too fucking hot."

I turned to face him, my hand reaching up and tucking his chestnut hair behind an ear. It was soft, silky. At odds with the disarray it appeared to be in. "Not to sound too cliché, but I think we should go somewhere more private."

Mateo made a sound of agreement before he was lifting me up with him and throwing me over his shoulder.

He ignored my protests and the concern of the patrons as he walked swiftly out the door.

His one hand holding my dress down and his other securing me in place.

"This wasn't what I had in mind!" I objected, trying to wriggle free.

He ignored me, walking a single block before pausing in front of a hotel. "Lucky I was staying nearby." He cast his attention left and right. "Someone has been following you," he murmured the words before walking into the hotel.

My irritation shifted to unease. It was hard to see anything other than Mateo's glorious ass as he walked us to the elevator, but his words were breaking through my drunken stupor.

Is it my stalker? Someone else? What if by being with Mateo he ends up involved? Anxiety prickled across my skin at the thought as Mateo stepped inside the elevator.

I was thankful to see the elevator's interior wasn't reflective.

I didn't want to even imagine what I looked like at this point. My messy hair, the rolls on my stomach pushing out the sheer fabric of the dress, the scars on my legs on full display.

"Can you let me down now please? This isn't the most comfortable."

He obliged. Sort of. Instead he lifted me so he was holding me up and forced me to wrap my legs around him. With the shortness of the dress, my cunt rubbed against him. Only a thin layer of silky material separating me from his jeans.

He grunted at the contact.

I could barely manage to get my legs around him as I used my arms to encircle his neck.

My eyes found his. "This works."

His face was an impenetrable mask, but his eyes were swirling with emotion.

Lust, excitement, *adoration*.

The elevator dinged and he walked us off; his attention torn between me and where we were going.

Only a few more steps and we were in a room.

I could tell Mateo appreciated my body, that he was impressed with what he saw. It was why being wrapped around this behemoth of a man made me feel so powerful, wanted, and *horny*. I wanted nothing more than to end my dry spell with him whether it was a good idea or not. I needed to let loose.

I deserved it.

Once he had the door shut, I yanked his head down, pressing my lips to his.

I could tell that I was drunk as fuck, but I didn't care. I wanted more of this man, of whatever he had to offer.

I wanted to fuck him and get it out of my system.

Pushing my tongue into his mouth, he allowed me to take control.

I lost myself for a moment into the feel of his hand under the curve of my ass holding me compressed to him. Of his other hand tangled in my hair as we consumed each other.

But when it was time to pull apart, I made the mistake of glancing around.

My eyes landed on the TV's black screen. Of my reflection.

My wild hair, my chubby cheeks, my arms falling out of the dress sleeves.

He wasn't expecting me to jump off him as I tumbled back onto the ground with an *umph*, but I didn't pause.

Finding my destination, I made my way to the bathroom, slamming and locking the door shut behind me.

It was time to puke up anything that was left in my stomach.

Chapter 7

MATEO

Mateo had never made a woman sick over a kiss before.

Seeing his bloodied hands? Sure.

Watching him dismember a man with a single weapon? Most definitely.

But kissing him? Well, he hadn't really kissed that many women, but they hadn't reacted like that before.

In fact, he had always suspected he might be asexual, but maybe that wasn't the case at all.

Because even with Yara's retching from the bathroom, his dick wouldn't go down. It was hard as steel as he adjusted it uncomfortably in his waistband, willing it to go limp.

He might kill men for a living, but he wasn't a monster. He wasn't going to be doing anything with his hard cock tonight.

Yara was clearly too intoxicated for any more than kissing.

Should he go check on her? Or would she rather be alone for this?

His phone ringing brought him out of his thoughts.

"Where the fuck are you and where is Yara?" Kazi's voice was just as annoying as he remembered. The pip squeak was a lucky son of a bitch though. His assignment had been to watch over this woman for years.

Mateo felt anger and jealousy course through him in equal strokes. "She's puking, too much to drink. But she'll be fine," he clipped out.

"Are you sure that's what it was? She has... she, well, is there anything that she could have seen herself on?" Kazi's fury was immediately replaced by concern, and it put Mateo on edge.

"What do you mean?" Mateo's tone turned threatening.

"Reflective surfaces. Mirror, metallic, anything she could see herself in?"

Mateo looked around the room and cursed when he found the TV. "What do I need to do?"

"Check on her. Cover the mirrors, don't make it obvious. Where are you? I'm coming."

Mateo debated his options, but realized the woman most likely would be comforted by Kazi's presence, and Kazi might actually be helpful. Maybe. "I will kill you with my bare hands if you make things worse." Mateo meant every word. "I'll text you, our location."

He didn't wait for a response before ending the call.

Chapter 8

D lifted his precious angel Yara's phone up and snapped a picture of the hotel she was just carried inside of before shutting it back off. *Wouldn't want to be tracked further than this.*

His blood was on fire, attempting to melt him from the inside out. It was time to teach her another fucking lesson. She was going too far.

He taught Yara better in their time together. She should have known not to come out here, to follow this silly dream of hers.

To change her name. To try to disappear from him.

For a while, he left her be, but then her face landed on the front page of a magazine.

It made it easy to find her. To track her down. To secure a job and start up a life here.

Except she wasn't getting the message. Wasn't reading the letters. Ignored his warnings.

Well, it seemed she just needed a reminder of what happened when she didn't listen to him.

He flexed his fists, slipped her phone back into his pocket, and walked away.

He would be kind and return it to Yara. Just not yet.

Chapter 9

MATEO

Yara was cradling the toilet as he broke the door to the bathroom down. He would pay for that... Probably.

She jumped a bit but didn't even look at him. "You can go. Can't you see that I'm in the middle of an appointment with the toilet?" she muttered out acerbically.

Ignoring her, Mateo glanced around the space. He found what he was looking for. Without pausing, he picked up a towel and wrapped it around his fist before punching the mirror.

"What the fuck are you doing?" Her words slurred a bit as she turned to him, tears rolling down her beautiful face, her hair a chaotic mess, and shining brightly through it all was a long jagged scar.

He had noticed it wasn't her only one. They painted her bare skin in unassuming places.

Brush strokes that made her into a beautiful piece of art.

Mateo decided it was his favorite part of her, evidence that she was just as broken as he knew himself to be. Except she was wrapped in a much prettier package than he was. And more importantly, he hated that she had gone through any suffering.

But now, he wanted to cover every scar of hers with a new memory. One that involved him.

His mind was at war with itself over the woman. He needed to clear it.

"Take a shower with me." He turned the water on before stepping forward to lift her up, she had lost her shoes at some point, and he didn't want her to step on any of the mirror's shards. At least that was the excuse he used internally.

He didn't wait for her reply, he stepped into the tub before lowering her down in his lap. The shower's mist hitting them from above had warmed up as they sat in the tub, both fully clothed.

"You'll ruin my dress," Yara weakly argued as she attempted to escape his hold, her shifting was causing his dick to stir, but he willed it to go down.

"Who cares?" he grumbled, leaning back, pulling her with him. "Close your eyes and just relax."

After a moment she acquiesced. "This is new," she murmured, looking up at him upside-down through her lashes, her head on his chest. "I've never gone to a hotel with a man to shower fully dressed." Her voice was saturated in sarcasm. She shifted, but this time it was into him more.

He wrapped his arms around her, kissing the top of her head. "You are too trusting, I could be a bad man. A murderer."

"Kazi is the only man I trust."

Mateo twitched underneath her in discontent.

"And he trusted me into your care, so by extension I trust you. Besides, he wouldn't allow someone around that would hurt me." Yara's hand found his and she began to trace lines up and down.

The hot water was still showering down on them, drenching their clothes, landing occasionally in Mateo's eyes, but he didn't care. He was entranced. Obsessed with her touch.

Of her little fingers as they painted lines along his skin. Of how instead of the disgust he usually felt at another person's touch, he was *enjoying* it.

Mateo thought back to her kissing him. The way her ridiculously petite body had melded itself to him, how her soft lips were at odds with the fierceness in her eyes. Yara might have been damaged and hurt in the past, but he could tell she had never been broken. That she was a capable woman.

Perhaps even strong enough to handle him?

Mateo was not a man of small measures. He did everything fiercely. Fully. Yara would be no different now that he had set his sights on her.

"What happened at dinner?" he asked the question that had been burning in his gut, that would decide the fate of the *pendejo* she left behind there.

"Liam? Just another man that thinks because I run a taboo dating site it means I'm easy. That I want to fuck every client." Yara laughed humorlessly.

Mateo had to force himself to not tighten his grip on the woman. He could tell she was fragile, tiny, small. Except she was also ferocious, and he didn't doubt she could take care of herself.

Key in on the man with the bloody nose at the bar. The sight had been enchanting. He wished nothing more than to see her beat any man that came near her again.

But she wouldn't need to anymore.

Mateo was here now.

And *Liam?* He would be dealing with the man himself.

She continued on, not noticing the change in Mateo's mood, his murderous intent.

"The fucking irony is I haven't even used my own site, haven't delved into my own *desires*. I'm twenty-eight years old and barely even having sex. I'm terrified of putting myself out there and trying what I'm curious about. I couldn't be a bigger hypocrite, constantly telling my bestie she needs to join it and explore herself, adventure into her interests. Meanwhile, here I am, not listening to my own advice. I think it's time to do something…someone." The last word was a husky whisper.

Mateo couldn't control his reaction, he squeezed Yara tighter to him, grumbling into her ear, "And what is it that you want to try, little bee?"

She said something under her breath, he wasn't quite sure he heard correctly.

He wanted to push her, have her say it again, but his eyes caught on the scars around her wrists. He hadn't noticed them before.

He readjusted his grip, his hand moving her wrist back and forth.

Icy cold dread dropped into his gut. "What are these from?" he asked gruffly.

She twisted uncomfortably until their eyes met, hers were glassy, unfocused. "Car accident." The lie was evident. "All of them are." She shifted back around, reaching forward and turning the water off. "It's time to let me out."

These weren't from a fucking car accident.

Who the fuck hurt this woman?

Anger and possession were worming their way into his skin, into his veins, into his blood. He hardly knew Yara, but he planned on changing that.

Chapter 10

KAZI

Kazi was seething. He had tried to track Yara's phone earlier, but the signal stopped at the restaurant, until it pinged back to life at this hotel, before disappearing again.

He had been out of his mind with worry the entire night, thinking he had made a mistake in leaving her with Mateo. That something bad had happened.

That her stalker had finally escalated as Kazi knew they would.

He was almost positive Yara knew exactly who it was, so why hadn't she told him?

His mind was a disarray of chaos as he pushed into the hotel room with the key the front desk had given him. Kazi wasn't sure what he expected to see, but it wasn't Mateo carrying a soaked Yara from the bathroom. Glancing around for any reflective items in the room, he found the TV broken on the floor.

"What the fuck?" Kazi hissed out before he could stop himself. He specifically said not to be *obvious*.

Mateo shrugged a shoulder.

Kazi thought Yara was sleeping, but she reached up a fist to punch Mateo. "Let me down you giant of a man. I hate being this far from the ground."

Kazi could tell she drank but decided against mentioning it. "I brought you some clothes from our house." He wouldn't mention how he had torn up half their home in anxiety.

Mateo carefully put Yara on her feet before stepping back and folding his arms. Kazi attempted to quell his rising anxiety from being in the same room as the other man. Mateo was a killer, a torturer, a *freak*.

Except Mateo was staring at Yara like she was the only thing in existence. His eyes tracking her every move.

And she was fucking oblivious.

Kazi returned his attention to the woman, he would worry about that later. "Here you go, Miss Yara, let me help you. I got your favorite clothes."

Yara's cerulean eyes brightened at his words. "What would I do without you Kazi?" She took the clothes from him and it took everything in him to not reach out. To not catch her hand and pull her to him. To push his lips against hers, show her how he felt. That he needed her.

Movement in Kazi's periphery pulled him from his yearning. Yara whipped her dress off, throwing it in Mateo's direction, before pulling the baggy sweatpants and long sleeve on.

"Yara." The warning in Mateo's tone was evident as he dropped her dress to the ground, but Yara ignored it.

Kazi's anxiety and frustration were causing painful piercing shocks along his skin. He couldn't reprimand her, she wouldn't listen.

Why was she trusting Mateo? Undressing in front of him?

Fully clothed, she turned around on wobbly feet. "Well, I guess I might as well stay here for the night. Also, Kazi, can you get me a new phone? I think I left mine at the restaurant."

A prickle of unease shot down his spine. "Are you sure?" he asked softly, frozen in place as he watched Yara make herself comfortable in the large bed, ignoring the broken TV entirely.

"Yep. You were right. Liam was another asshole." The words came out blearily as she blinked her eyes slowly for a few moments before they didn't open again. It wasn't but a minute later that he could just make out her light snoring.

That was one skill set she excelled in, sleeping whenever or wherever she could. Kazi suspected it was from years of being forced to, years of abuse.

He clenched his fists in anger as he thought about how her trauma affected her. She rarely ate, she was littered with scars, couldn't stand her own reflection, and it took him years to finally convince her to sleep on a bed with him. Before that, when they first lived together, she would end up in her closet more nights than he cared to admit.

He didn't realize how badly she was hurting for far too long; he wouldn't make that mistake again.

Even if she wouldn't tell him what was wrong, he would get it out of her one way or another.

"What happened to her?" Mateo's deep voice jumped Kazi out of his trance and he looked back at the man.

"You can leave now, I've got her." Kazi did his best to sound stern, he didn't like where this was heading. He didn't like the glint in Mateo's eyes, the determination in his voice.

Mateo sounded exactly like he did when he found a new *project* to fixate on. Those projects always ended up worse for wear. Well that wasn't exactly correct. They always ended up dead or damaged beyond repair. Kazi may not physically be around the *family*, but that did nothing to abate the rumors of Mateo's cruelties.

Of his history of torture and murder.

"I don't think I will. I already let Emilio know that I would be sticking around. You didn't mention that the stalker was escalating. Someone followed her from the restaurant, to a bar, and then here. And they were good, I couldn't catch them." Mateo pushed off the wall walking towards the bed, shedding his shirt as he went.

"What are you doing?"

"Sleeping with her," Mateo stated as he got into the bed.

"No the fuck you aren't. Leave her alone." Kazi was channeling all of his inner rage to challenge this man as he got in on the other side of the bed.

"Shut up you two!" Yara shot up in a half sleep state, scaring the ever-loving shit out of Kazi. He was used to her sleep talking, but he hadn't been expecting it. "Just both stay here with me," she grumbled as she fell back onto the bed.

"She's an interesting woman." Mateo snuggled against her side, wrapping a beefy arm around her.

"No, she's not interesting, you're not intrigued. Next, you're going to say 'she's not like other girls.' She doesn't need that. She is Miss Yara, and she deserves better than your hyper-fixation." Kazi was grasping at straws, but he knew he had fucked up.

"You're probably right, but it's too late for that. I have decided this will be my new mission. To keep her safe, to rid her of her stalker."

Apprehension rose up Kazi's throat, he swallowed it down as he settled in on the other side of Yara. He didn't know Mateo that well, but there was one thing he was certain of: Mateo always completed his missions.

Meaning from this moment on, Mateo would be a part of their lives.

Kazi just hoped that there would be enough space for the both of them.

Chapter 11

YARA

Waking up, I blinked my eyes blearily and stared up at the ceiling. The room was too fucking bright, and I felt like a used tampon. Disgusting, needing a change, and to be thrown away.

Ew.

Never drinking again.

The lie swirled through my mind as I attempted to get up, except I was locked down by restraints. Before the panic settled in, I turned my head and found Kazi's face, his long lashes, his eyes closed in sleep.

I almost shut my own again, but then I realized there were too many restraints and something warm pressing into my other side.

"You're awake." The familiar deep husky voice was muffled by my hair, but a moment later I was being yanked away from Kazi.

"Mateo," I acknowledged while he settled me on top of him, my hands landing on his bare chest. Straddling him stretched my legs almost to the point of pain, but I ignored it. His deep mahogany eyes were pulsing with emotion.

"You remember my name." He grinned up at me, shifting his hold until one hand gripped my hip bone and the other swept my hair back. "I was afraid you would forget it."

The daylight was streaming into the room, and with it, I was able to fully take in Mateo's appearance. That he was clearly a bit older, that there was darkness swirling in his eyes, that scars littered his face. On him, the scars didn't look like imperfections, instead they were accessories he wore. He was incredibly handsome and being on top of him was causing unwanted feelings to stir in my gut.

For the second time in as many days, I found someone new I was uncharacteristically attracted to.

A short beard covered his strong jawline, and I reached a hand absentmindedly to stroke it. The scratchiness tickling the pads of my fingers.

His face darkened. "Be careful Yara."

His words knocked me out of the trance I had fallen into and I went to jump off of him, but in doing so, my arm hit his.

I hissed in pain. "What did I do?" I couldn't recall hurting myself and the long sleeve I wore was covering the area.

Mateo's eyes darkened. "Cut your arm."

I remembered most everything from last night, but that incident was not coming to the front of my mind.

I would have to investigate the injury later.

"Well…" I drew the word out. "It was nice to meet you, but I really need to get into work, I have a million things to do. I guess I'll catch you around." I lifted my fist up.

"What are you doing?" He raised an eyebrow.

With my other hand, I grabbed his bulky arm and raised it before sliding to his hand. I folded his fingers until he formed a fist and then tapped it with my own. "Fist bumping you?" The duh was evident in my tone.

He began to shake under me, his eyes crinkling in laughter, leading to crows feet that further showed his older age. "Can't say I've used my fist like that before."

"Fucking hilarious, come here Miss Yara, let's get you off the big scary man." Kazi was officially awake and tugged me off of Mateo into his arms, hugging me lightly from behind.

It wasn't anything new, Kazi lived with me and oftentimes, if I had a nightmare or couldn't sleep, I would crawl into his bed. I did it so much that eventually we got rid of the second bed altogether.

"So how are you cousins exactly?" They looked literally nothing alike.

"My fathe—"

"His sis—"

They began to speak at the same time.

"Uhuh." I wriggled out of Kazi's arms. "So, 'cousins.' Alrighty then." I got up off the bed and scanned the room for my shoes. "What happened to the TV?"

Kazi and Mateo exchanged a look this time before talking, Kazi gave a slight shake. "You knocked into it, it's how you cut your arm."

I surveyed them both, definitely a lie, but whatever. I needed to get going. "Sure. And my shoes?"

Kazi pointed to the door. "There's a new pair along with a replacement phone at the door for you. The new phone should be programmed and ready to go."

I offered him a genuine smile. "You know you are the best assistant a girl could ask for?"

"I aim to please, Miss Yara."

I went down a hallway to the door and sure enough, right inside were two bags.

When I returned to the men, they were both dressed.

"Here, I'll swing you by the house to get ready and refreshed," Kazi offered.

"Sounds good, well bye then Mr. Mateo."

Kazi appeared uncomfortable for a minute before stepping into my space and steering me back towards the door. "He's going to be sticking around."

I started to protest. Sure, I would have fucked Mateo last night, but that didn't mean I wanted to see him every day. I may be more comfortable around him than I ought to be but that was it. That wasn't a ticket into my life.

Kazi saw my trepidation and cut me off before I could argue. "He works as a bodyguard back home. He's going to stay until we figure out the stalker situation."

The air whooshed out of my lungs. I was doing my best to actively forget about that. Especially since I could guess who the quote-unquote stalker was. "Fine," I agreed begrudgingly.

I could tell when Kazi wouldn't let something go, he was a stubborn fucker It was what I loved about him.

But in this moment, I was beginning to hate it too.

Chapter 12

YARA

It had been a week since my first encounter with Mateo, and I was currently doing something I tried to actively avoid as best I could. Staring at my reflection. Except I was examining my arm, pointedly ignoring the rest of my body.

Specifically, the bandage covering the gash on my arm. I wracked my brain for the umpteenth time trying to recollect the incident. I remembered the rest of the night, but for the life of me, I couldn't recall injuring myself.

The cut was directly over my birth control implant. For a sick moment, when I first saw it, I thought I may have somehow managed to remove it, but after rubbing the area, I could tell there was still something in my arm.

It was mostly healed now, and I secured the bandage back into place, re-covering the mirror. I could tell it was going to scar.

Another imperfection.

I shut the entire line of thought down as I stepped out of the bathroom, it was connected to my office, and I was grateful to see that no one else was in it.

Since waking up in that hotel room, Mateo had not been more than fifteen feet from me at any point.

It was aggravating.

At least that's what I was trying to convince myself, except I found that I was enjoying his attention.

His intense unwavering gaze, his calming aura, the way he ignored the rest of the world except for me.

It made me feel special in some twisted way. Being around him had me dressing up for him, just to see his reaction. He made me feel confident, beautiful, *wanted*.

The only problem was that I knew he didn't buy my car accident story and every time he saw a new scar, something akin to rage skittered across the man's face. I knew it was only a matter of time before he pushed me, and I wasn't ready for it when he did.

Settling down into my chair, I caught my reflection for a moment before logging into my computer. The self-deprecating thoughts did not assault me today, and I was incredibly grateful for it.

Pulling up my email, I switched to the account I made for something specific.

A quiver of excitement shot down my spine.

Even with all the chaos that seemed to saturate my life, I was determined to do something for myself. To delve into my own darkest desires. And the older man with the breeding kink and sage green eyes? Well, I knew inherently it had to be with him.

After debating back and forth and doing my own background check, I sent him an email yesterday, and today, I received his reply.

I wanted to make sure he was onboard before taking things any further with him, before I let him know I was the party he would be matched with.

My eyes scanned the email reading it.

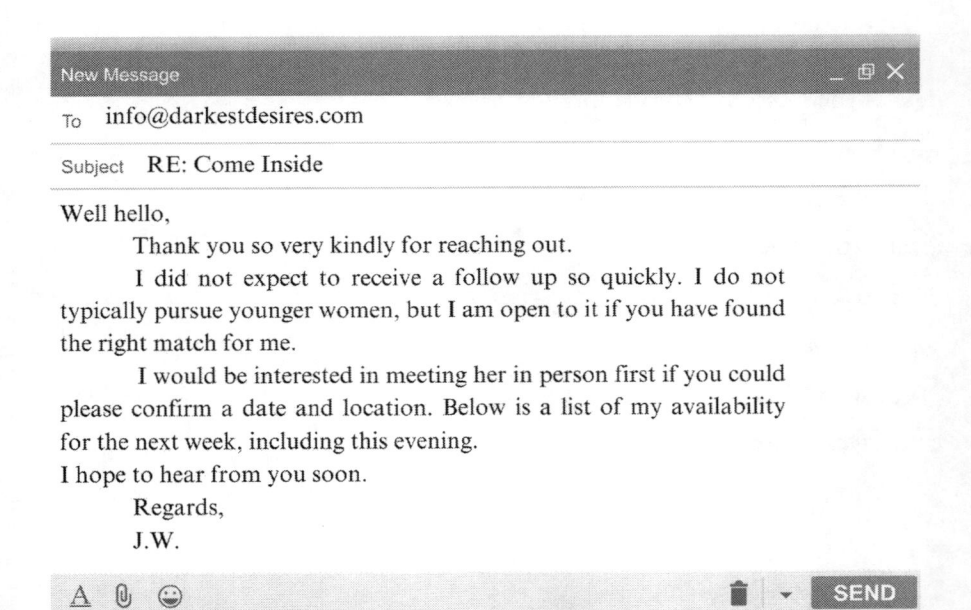

> **New Message**
>
> **To** info@darkestdesires.com
>
> **Subject** RE: Come Inside
>
> Well hello,
>   Thank you so very kindly for reaching out.
>   I did not expect to receive a follow up so quickly. I do not typically pursue younger women, but I am open to it if you have found the right match for me.
>   I would be interested in meeting her in person first if you could please confirm a date and location. Below is a list of my availability for the next week, including this evening.
> I hope to hear from you soon.
>   Regards,
>   J.W.

My heart beat rapidly in my chest as I scanned his availability and typed out my reply. I had just enough time to hit send before Mateo returned to my office, coffee in hand.

"As requested." He walked slowly around my desk. Standing behind me he reached over my shoulder to set the coffee down, his woodsy scent filling my nostrils as he lingered there for a few moments too long.

Kazi took that moment to walk in, a scowl forming on his face. "Mateo," he uttered exasperatedly.

Mateo chuckled before lifting back up to his full impressive height and stepping back.

"Well now that you're both here, I have something to tell you." I turned in my chair to face Mateo, but didn't realize how close he still was until my knees landed against him.

He leaned down into my space, putting his hands on my chair, his face inches from mine. His liquid brown eyes were flickering with emotion, but I couldn't quite discern which ones.

He bent lower until his lips found my ear, his tongue lashing out, licking up its length.

I shivered back against my chair before gaining my bearings. I moved my arms up, pushing him away and attempting to regain my composure.

"Mmm, I love that you're playing hard to get," Mateo grumbled out.

He had been pushing at me every day, trying to get under my skin. I wanted to say I hated it.

But I didn't.

I was *enjoying* it.

Too much.

Which was another reason I needed to follow through with my plans. He was Kazi's "cousin." Maybe they weren't blood related, but I shouldn't get involved. When I was drunk, I wasn't thinking clearly, I just wanted to climb the man, but here in the light of day? I knew better.

I wouldn't lose Kazi over a night of fun. Whether it be with Kazi himself or someone he was tied to.

Kazi pushed Mateo aside looking down at me in concern. "You have that look on your face," he stated worriedly.

"And which one is that?" I raised an eyebrow.

"You know exactly which one—where you are about to tell me something that you shouldn't do, but you already have your mind made up." His lips flattened into a line, and his hand went up to tousle his hair. It was a nervous tick of his.

I snorted. "Okay we might spend too much time together. But yes, I have another discretion package tonight." The lie slid out easily; I couldn't exactly tell them I was meeting a man for myself.

Kazi went to protest, but I held up my hand.

"It's not going to be like last time, I *promise*. And I am already aware one of you will be joining me. Just don't intervene and please don't eavesdrop like I know you always try to do." I narrowed my eyes at Kazi. I knew there would be no way around him being there, but I didn't need them both. "Mateo, you're staying behind though."

"No, the fuck I'm not."

I turned my attention to him. "Liam was a one-off situation, but I can't have you staring holes into my head every time I go on one of these *dates*, you weren't exactly subtle last time."

"Well, you shouldn't be going on these fucking dates at all, why Kazi allows you—"

I cut Mateo off, leveling him with my frostiest stare. "Kazi doesn't *allow* me to do anything. This is *my* company that I built on my own blood, sweat, and rage. I am a grown ass adult woman that doesn't need to be told what to do. And you are brand fucking new in my life. Do I think you're hot? Yes. But do not take *me* letting *you* be around as my acceptance. You are only here on Kazi's wishes. The second I decide it's too much, you're fucking gone."

"I just want to keep you safe," Mateo grumbled.

"Yeah, I fucking get that and that's why you haven't been kicked to the curb yet, but you're going to have to trust me. I made it this many years without you, I can make it one night with just Kazi."

Mateo heaved out a sigh, before curling his lips up smugly. "You think I'm hot?"

My head fell into my hands in exasperation. "Fucking men! Get out! I need to get dressed."

Chapter 13

J.W.

J.W. shifted at the table, tapping his foot. He had a million other things to do, but he carved a space out of his endless work to be here. He needed a reprieve and found himself more excited than he had any right to be.

J.W. knew the woman he was meeting was going to be younger, but he wasn't aware of the exact difference. The employee had sent over her profile, background, and interests.

The kink that she was most interested in.

Everything except her exact age and a picture.

So here he was at a booth in a corner of a hotel restaurant he had never frequented before, waiting for his *date*, fiddling with his watch impatiently. He had arrived twenty minutes early in his haste, and now he was forced to linger for her.

Movement in his periphery drew his attention, his brow creased.

He was familiar with the beautiful woman that ran *Darkest Desires*, but he couldn't understand why she was the one meeting him... Unless his original match declined.

Irritation simmered under his skin.

A waste of time.

He stood up to greet her.

"Hello..." He took her hand, squeezing it lightly. He wasn't exactly sure what to call her.

He had only seen pictures of the woman prior. She was much smaller in person. She looked up at him through her lashes offering a striking smile. "Call me Yara, please." She removed her hand from his, leaving a frigid emptiness behind. She gestured to the table. "Have a seat."

J.W. was disgruntled but didn't argue with the woman. He was still shocked by her appearance. Yara was well known in this town, except she was rarely seen out in public.

J.W. rigidly sat back down. He wasn't accustomed to following anyone's lead, but he found himself wanting to listen to her.

Yara took the space across from him. J.W. shifted agitatedly in his seat waiting for the woman to say something.

Anything.

Yara was a surprise. He was impatient and beginning to suspect this had in fact been a waste of his time, money, and energy.

"So how about this weather?" He threw out his go-to small talk line after she still didn't speak.

Yara hummed, glancing around, staring out the window that took up an entire wall behind him. It was pitch-black outside.

"Was my match not able to make it?" he asked carefully after another moment, attempting to keep the disdain out of his voice and adjusting a cufflink.

"Not exactly." The woman heaved a sigh and finally met his eyes.

For a moment he couldn't breathe.

He was drowning.

Her eyes were beautiful, but it was the pain, the evidence of a lifetime of struggle reflected in their depths that had him clenching his fists.

It reminded him of his own eyes, it was why he so easily recognized it.

They were *haunted*. Listless. Teetering on the cusp of broken.

What in the hell has this woman been through?

He was feeling needlessly outraged on her behalf. He didn't understand his visceral reaction to this woman.

To this much *younger* woman.

His attention shifted up and found a particularly long scar across her forehead.

Fury pulsated up his spine, skittered along his skin, settled into his stomach. A fiery rage he wasn't sure how to put out or exactly where the feelings manifested from.

Except, that wasn't true.

He couldn't deny it, he was invested in Yara's story, in what had happened to her.

He had an inherent need to know more about her, to understand what cruelties this world had pushed this woman through.

What is she doing to him?

Yara shifted uncomfortably, adjusting her hair, letting it fall forward to cover the scar.

J.W. watched as she squared her shoulders, narrowed her eyes, and physically transformed before him into a confident, threatening, businesswoman.

It was eerie watching the mask slide itself into place.

"I am your match." Her attention was focused over his shoulder still, out the window. "If you agree to it." Without looking she pulled a folder out of the briefcase he hadn't observed prior.

He was too busy examining the woman herself.

He had lowered his guard, not noticing every piece of information he could.

It was a trick that got him ahead in his career.

If only it had worked the same in his personal life. If only he had seen the signs.

J.W. shut down that line of thought.

He was uncharacteristically drawn to this woman, so much so it took longer than he cared to admit to realize what she had said. "You?" he cracked out. His heart pounded a painful beat in his chest. He swallowed thickly, reaching for his glass of water and chugging a few gulps before straightening his shoulders and adjusting his tie.

Is his business partner—the man that recommended this site—setting him up for some sick joke?

"You?" This time the word came out stiffly.

"Mr. Wright, if you could please look through the folder. At the bottom is where you can sign. Due to the," she paused folding her hands, "*nature* of my proposition, you would be refunded your payment for our services."

He stared at the woman; he couldn't deny he was interested in her, but she was *too* young.

"I can see the indecision warring across your face. So, how about this? We have dinner, you think on it, and at the end of our meal we can go our separate ways?" She smiled at him before glancing over her shoulder and then returning her attention to him.

His attention found who she was looking at. A man was staring unblinkingly their way.

He knew enough about her company to also know about the infamous Kazi. The man was never more than ten feet from Yara.

J.W. weighed his options. He hadn't really put himself out there in years and the woman before him was sexier than he had expected, her smile lighting up her face in an almost iridescent way.

Additionally, he didn't really have the time to go out on the socially acceptable number of dates to fuck, and he really needed to get laid. Typically, he stuck to keeping his company running and staying as busy as possible to forget the tragedy that hit him years ago, but he could tell he needed something to give. The stress had been affecting him more than he cared to admit, and his business partner had noticed.

Hence, this meeting.

J.W. forced himself to relax his shoulders, releasing some of the tension stored there.

Yara was watching him with a pensive gaze, her lips pursed into the remnants of a pout.

He appraised Yara again. She was an objectively beautiful woman that was showing clear interest in him.

That wanted him to fuck her.

To breed her. To fill her with his cum and use her as he pleased.

"So"–she raised an eyebrow, gesturing at the table–"dinner?"

It was really a no brainer, he was already here, he might as well enjoy it. "With pleasure."

To say he was intrigued would be an understatement, but even more than that? He couldn't stop imagining her stomach swollen, pregnant with his child.

He shifted uncomfortably in his seat. His first and only long-term relationship had ruined any plans of future children. The vasectomy was evidence of that.

But even still, a man could dream. Could fantasize.

Chapter 14

YARA

I hadn't laughed this much in years. I wasn't sure how this was going to go when I first got here.

The man seemed like a bit of an ass, but now that we had split a meal, shared intimate parts of our lives, and dropped the stiffness of business acquaintances?

I could tell he wasn't an asshole. He was just lonely.

And he had been, for a very, *very* long time.

My background check had yielded quite a bit of information on him...in his work life at least. He owned a very large agency that had landed several well-known clients.

He had a silent partner that assisted in his endeavors, but otherwise, his work seemed pretty straightforward, and his personal life wasn't marred with any blemishes.

"Were you ever married? I couldn't find anything on a wife, but you must have had someone over the years?"

He stiffened before forcing a smile, except his face was devoid of light. "I was never married, but I had a long-time partner back when I was much younger. She is actually the one that had me get the vasectomy." He reached to grab the wine bottle, topping us both off. "And what about your story Yara?" His eyes wore holes into mine.

I shifted uncomfortably in my seat, tipping my glass up, and chugging the wine down in several large gulps.

I gazed right back at him, not blinking. "Do you ever feel as if you are staring at a different person in the mirror every time you look?"

His eyes widened in surprise; whatever he expected me to say, it wasn't that, but then he set his fork down and brought a long finger to his lips in contemplation. "I try not to look in mirrors too often, because they aren't an accurate representation of who I am. But yes, sometimes I do find myself thinking I am a fraud. My company would have gone under without my backer. He randomly stumbled upon me one day about ten years ago. I was already based in California, but he pushed me to move to this area." He reached up brushing his hair back from his face and my eyes followed the move.

My nerves were static. I was trying to portray myself as calm, but inside a fire was burning.

This man was more than I bargained for.

"What's your story, Yara? What sent you all the way out here?" I watched his attention fall to my wrists.

Sometimes strangers would rudely comment on the scars there. About the obvious evidence of being bound for a long period of time.

Now that I owned this company most suspected it was part of my own *depravity*.

But occasionally, I would meet a person that didn't think that.

That recognized they weren't left voluntarily.

Izzy was the first, but she never pushed me. Just like I didn't with her fear of heights.

Even best friends could keep secrets from each other.

Other times, I would get interrogated on the matter. Like by Kazi and Mateo, the questions burning in their eyes every time they found a new scar.

It made me uncomfortable. It added to the list of reasons why I shouldn't cross the line with either of them.

But there was an indescribable urge to relinquish my inner demons onto *this* man. This practical stranger. I imagined his sturdy shoulders could handle their weight.

"I'll tell you what." Our plates had long since been cleared, and I used the empty space to open the folder to the first page of the packet. "Sign the NDA, I'll sign mine, and then I will tell you whatever you want to know."

I could see the intrigue flicker across his face, his lip quirking up in a half smile. "The catch?" He chuckled in a deep vibrating baritone.

The sound went directly to my cunt. My hand reached across the table to stroke his, my eyes finding his. "Sign the NDA and I'll tell you what you want, but it means you're interested. That by the end of tonight you're going to be pumping me full with your cum."

I gasped in surprise as he snatched my hand with his free one faster than I could see. His long calloused fingers encircled my wrist. I expected for terror to pierce me, but it didn't. It was instead a dark pleasure that rolled across my nerves.

He applied pressure, just on the cusp of pain.

"What if I hurt you? What if I'm not what you expected? What if I force you on your knees and make you work for it?" His voice turned guttural, saturated in desire.

Each question sent a volt of electricity straight to my throbbing core. The dinner had been tame, but now with his full attention, I was beginning to unravel. "I can handle it."

With his fingers still shackling my wrist, his other moved to the pen on the table.

His eyes never left mine. "You're going to ruin me." He bit out each word as he signed the document, finally releasing my wrist.

I reached for the folder, signing mine, and discreetly showing him before closing it back and setting it to the side.

"You asked for my story?" My eyes found a scar on my forearm, another on my palm, a third on the back of my hand. I poured us both another glass from the wine bottle, it was running precariously low at this point. "I may seem like an angelic woman that has had it easy, and maybe for the most part I have, but that wasn't always the case."

My attention landed on him. He was following my every word, giving me his full attention.

I wasn't sure if I was happy about that or wished he would tell me to stop.

I knew Kazi had been watching us, but he wouldn't eavesdrop. He knew better.

"When I was eight years old, I was adopted by a loving couple and relocated to Florida, but before that? Before that I lived with a monster."

Others referred to him by his name. But me? I called him dad.

Chapter 15

YARA

I closed my eyes allowing the memories to flood me. Thankfully, they were beginning to fade, but sometimes in the dead of night, I would wake up in Kazi's arms sweating and trembling.

"What happened?" The concern coating my dinner companion's voice was what kept me grounded in the here and now.

"What do you think it takes to be beautiful?" I muttered the words out hoarsely, my gaze flashing up to meet his.

His brow crinkled in unease. "I can't say I have ever thought about it." His expression turned wistful, he rolled his lower lip into his mouth, biting it. "Sometimes I don't think beauty is outward at all. It's how you choose to be despite everything else."

I cackled, an unhinged noise that left me on its own accord. "I think you and I both know how shallow this world is. You're an agent. You know that beauty sells." My fingers traced a particularly nasty scar up my forearm. "He used to say, *'Scars can be covered, but your ugliness can't,'* as he punished me for not being his idea of beauty. As he shackled me to the floor for days. As he withheld food and screamed profanities my way. It never took much to set him off. If I ever even had a single strand of hair out of place." I reached up patting it down.

"He?" The word left his lips in a harsh grating tone. His face coated in shadows.

"The monster." I leveled him with my gaze. "Father dearest."

The air left him in a whoosh. "Your father? What kind of man? Fuck!"

"He's dead now, but his impact? It hasn't faded too much unfortunately."

He brought a hand up to rub his temple. "Yara, I know this may not mean much coming from a practical stranger, but we make our own beauty. Sure, you are undeniably gorgeous, but it's more than that. You are vibrant, you have brought life into every moment since we met. But even more importantly? No one else's opinion matters except your own."

"But that's the thing, isn't it?" I went to reach for my wine, but he caught my hand, holding it in a tight grip, addicting static fire spread through my nerves while I tried to ignore it. "How does one build confidence after years of that? And then when I thought I finally might be okay. That I might finally accept who I was as a person, flaws and all, a particularly nasty man fell into my life."

Daniel.

I laughed caustically. "In some ways he was even worse. The scars he left behind were just as painful."

I leaned back against my chair, watching his face the entire time. There wasn't any pity present, just fury.

"So that's my story, a twice broken girl trying to figure out her shit one faltering step at a time. And that's why I'm here." I squeezed his hand back, ignoring the fluttering of emotions he was causing.

How I somehow felt more seen in his presence than I had in years.

"You're not broken," he argued.

I waved a hand in dismissal, but internally, my heart pounded against my ribcage.

"So, James, do you want to tell me your story now? Or do you want to do it after?"

"After," he practically growled out the word.

"Okay, well first things first. I need to lose my *guard*." I didn't look behind me, I could still feel the holes Kazi was burrowing into the back of my head. "Here's the plan."

Chapter 16

D

His Doll. His Yara.

D fidgeted in annoyance, he had stayed out of sight in this disgusting restaurant, but their dinner had gone on for ages.

His doll was acting differently than she should.

D wasn't quite sure of the specifics, but he knew for certain this wasn't going according to plan. He had signed James up for this, knew he would request the discretion package, but why did it seem like more than that?

This date had gone on for too long; he wasn't sure what there was left to discuss.

Why did it almost appear they were *flirting?*

A moment later she threw her drink at James. His anger simmered down, and he chuckled.

Better.

"Fuck off!" his doll screeched loudly enough to echo around the entire restaurant.

Silence followed for a moment before the hum of conversation started up again. He kept his eyes focused on her retreat, she was heading for the bathrooms.

The time wasn't right to take her, she had caused too much of a scene.

He would need to wait a little longer, he would have to make James meet up with her again. Get her in public. Further away from Kazi.

D glanced back at James, a restaurant employee was leading him away, blubbering apologies.

D had seen enough, it was time to leave.

Time to work on an alternate plan.

D was a patient man, but even still, he couldn't stamp down his excitement.

His doll would be returning to him soon.

Whether she wanted to or not.

Chapter 17

YARA

Slamming the bathroom door shut, I locked it behind me.

Not a moment later, I heard footsteps approaching.

"Yara, are you okay?" The worry in Kazi's tone almost made me feel guilty.

But I deserved this. I needed this. And he wouldn't understand.

I didn't respond. I counted down from one hundred as he banged on the door. Finally I pulled out my phone, sending a blank text to Izzy. She already knew the plan. We had discussed it earlier when I sent Mateo for coffee.

I heard Kazi's phone ringing a moment later. "What do you mean she's getting a cab? I just saw her run into the bathroom?!" A pause. "Jumped through a window? What the fuck is Yara up to? Why didn't you stop her?" Another pause. "Oh fuck don't cry! Shit, I'm sorry. I didn't mean it. Don't tell Yara!"

His voice was growing more distant as he spoke. Izzy always could throw on the water works when needed.

I owed her after this.

I waited just a few more minutes before grabbing my bag and hightailing it out of the restroom. I didn't even look around. I simply ran to the stairs I had spotted earlier.

This restaurant was conveniently located in a hotel.

A hotel that I had a room for.

Before I started the fake fight with James, I gave him a copy of the room card and told him I needed an hour.

That hour was down to forty-five minutes when I finally stepped into the room.

Opening my briefcase, I pulled the folder out. I had labeled it myself.

Come Inside

I chuckled as I read through the documents. I always did like a good pun.

Welcome to your Darkest Desires

IF YOU ARE READING THIS, YOU HAVE FINALLY TAKEN THE PLUNGE TO SATISFY YOUR NEEDS.
CONGRATULATIONS. WE ARE PROUD OF YOU. THERE IS NO NEED TO FEEL SHAME.
YOUR SATISFACTION AND SAFETY ARE OUR TOP PRIORITIES. ON THE NEXT PAGE YOU WILL CONFIRM WE HAVE CORRECTLY MARKED YOUR BOUNDARIES. WE WANT TO ENSURE THAT NOTHING GOES AWRY.

THERE WILL BE A PLACE TO PUT YOUR SAFEWORD. THIS WORD WILL BE USED BY YOUR PARTNER, OR PARTNERS, AS WELL.

IF YOU HAVE SELECTED TO KNOW YOUR PARTNER PRIOR, YOU WILL RECEIVE THEIR SUMMARY BELOW.

IF YOU HAVE SELECTED TO GO INTO THIS BLIND, YOU WILL NOT BE PROVIDED WITH ANY OF THEIR INFORMATION, BUT PLEASE REST ASSURED THAT THEY ARE A MATCH FOR YOU.

YOUR PARTNER, OR PARTNERS, HAVE BEEN THOROUGHLY VETTED AND TESTED. THEY WENT THROUGH THE SAME PROCESS YOU DID.

WE HOPE THIS TURNS INTO EXACTLY WHAT YOU WISH IT TO BE.

Reading through the document that I wrote so many years ago brought a bit of warmth to my heart, but did nothing to ease my anxiety.

This was real. I was doing this.

No turning back now.

Boundaries

PLEASE NOTE THAT THIS IS NOT A COMPLETE LIST, THIS IS ONLY WHAT WAS INPUT ON YOUR PROFILE. IF YOU HAVE ANYTHING SPECIFICALLY YOU WISH FOR YOUR PARTNER(S) TO PARTICIPATE IN, PLEASE CIRCLE IT ON THIS PAGE. YOU CAN REQUEST YOUR PARTNER(S) COMPLETE SOMETHING NOT LISTED, BUT THAT IS AT THEIR DISCRETION. ANY ITEMS ON THE DENIED LIST WILL BE RESPECTED.

ACCEPTED
- USING SEX TOYS, VIBRATORS, OR DILDOS, WITH A PARTNER
- PRAISE
- VAGINAL & BUTT PLUGS
- BREEDING
- ANAL INTERCOURSE
- VAGINAL INTERCOURSE
- ORAL SEX, VAGINAL
- FREE USE—CNC
- SPANKING
- ROLEPLAY—CNC
- ROLEPLAY—FORCED BREEDING

DENIED
- FISTING
- DVP & DAP
- RESTRAINTS & BLINDFOLDS

SAFEWORD:_____
ADDITIONAL INFORMATION: _____

I had quite a few I wanted to try this go round. But first things first, I filled out my safeword.

Scuttlebutt.

My cunt was throbbing in anticipation as I circled three of the lines above.

Breeding.

Vaginal & butt plugs.

Praise.

I needed to finish the liability portion. I took pictures of the signed NDAs and this document and uploaded it all to our secure portal. I then sent a copy to James.

> Me: I'll be in the shower. Toys are on the nightstand.

Casting my attention around the room, I found that everything was set up exactly how I requested.

The TV had been removed, the toys sat on the nightstand, and stepping to the dresser, I found several changes of clothes.

Buzzing caught my attention. Kazi had been blowing up my phone since I made it into the room, and Mateo was now joining forces to not let up.

I created a group chat and sent a text.

> Me: I'm safe. I'll call in the morning.

Shutting my phone off, I walked to the bathroom and was happy to see the mirror had been taken down.

The hotel was happy to oblige, I sent a substantial portion of my clients their way. And while sex work was typically frowned upon, dates that ended in sex were not.

I didn't have the time to spiral into that hypocrisy.

Turning on the shower, I stripped out of my clothes as it heated up.

I dug deep, pushing down all of my insecurities. All the voices in my head telling me how disgusting I looked.

How every part of me was ugly.

I thought about Mateo, of the way that I affected him. Of the way I caught Kazi staring at me when he thought I didn't notice.

Of how James had been entranced in my presence.

Maybe these flaws of mine had been made a million times worse by my own voice.

I would have to unpack that later.

Instead, I stepped under the shower's now hot mist, I still wasn't sure if this was a mistake or not.

I was anxious. Nervous. *Excited*.

This plan had seemed better on paper, but I wouldn't be turning back now.

Too stubborn for all that.

By the end of the night, I would be filled with cum.

By a man twice my age.

Chapter 18

MATEO

Mateo wiped his hands before answering the phone.

"I need you to check her tracker. Or give me access like I told you to do days ago." Kazi's voice was more grating than usual.

"What did you do?" Mateo spit the words into the phone, casting a glance at his current project.

"She seemed to get into an altercation with the man she was on a date with and then her friend, Izzy, called me, but I think they set me up. Yara's missing."

Mateo cursed under his breath, he pulled his knife free from the leg it currently resided in.

Muffled screaming filled the space.

"What are you doing?" Unease filtered through Kazi's worried tone.

"Handling the trash as promised. He was more than happy to meet at Yara's apartment."

Mateo, against his wishes, hadn't been staying with Kazi and Yara for the last week, but that didn't mean he couldn't find a way into their home.

It was almost too easy.

Imagine his surprise when he found it wasn't a two bedroom.

That they shared a bedroom.

It had sent him into a murderous rage, and he needed to let off some steam.

A particularly loud noise startled him out of his thoughts. "Shut up! The neighbors will get worried!" Mateo chastised the blubbering man.

The trash—Liam—was tied down onto the singular bed, spread eagle. They had already had quite some fun in the last hour, and the man was most likely just on the edge of passing out, but Mateo was about over it.

The noise did not lessen.

"I warned you." He struck his hand out, slicing a clean line across his neck.

Kazi was making annoying noises in his ear. Maybe they were words, but Mateo didn't have the energy to listen.

Mateo stood up to his full height, stretching as he went. He secured his knife back onto his person. "Yes, yes I hear you Kazi. But the fact of the matter is I don't care. You shouldn't have kept your living arrangements from me. And now you've lost our girl." Mateo hated that Kazi was stuck with her, but he could tell how much she needed him. Mateo could accept the bug if only for her sake.

He glanced down, Liam's blood was still flowing freely.

"It looks like you might have lost your apartment, too. Well, at least the bed." Mateo watched as crimson seeped into the mattress. "Call a clean-up crew. I'll find her with the tracker."

"I told you to leave in her birth control implant. Why did you replace it with the tracker?" Kazi muttered out.

"Because she might notice a new piece of plastic in her arm." Mateo tried to keep the sarcasm out of his tone.

He was worried Yara had gone missing, but the tracker would lead him back to her. And if anyone hurt her between now and then?

He cast his attention to the dead body below him.

Well, he could always take care of it.

Chapter 19

J.W.

James could hear the shower running as he stepped into the hotel room, shutting and locking it behind him.

His dick, which he had finally gotten under control at dinner, had hardened back to steel when Yara sent him over what she wanted, and it hadn't gone down since.

To say he was ready was an understatement.

But he wanted more than that. He wanted to leave his mark on Yara. Wanted her to return to him again and again.

Because he could already tell. She was a drug. An addiction. He hadn't wanted to cross the line because of her age, but even after their short time together, he inherently knew. She was what he had been looking for.

They had inexplicable chemistry. And the intelligence and depth to her? He would never be bored in her presence.

He cast a glance around the hotel room, finding the toys they would be using tonight.

Scuttlebutt. That was her safeword. He would adhere to it, but he hoped she wouldn't need it.

That she would like what he had to offer.

He loosened his tie and made quick work of shedding all of his clothes. He dimmed the lights, grabbed one of the sex toys, and without further ado, made his way to the bathroom.

Opening the door, he stopped dead in his tracks.

She was faced away from him in the shower, but the door was made of clear glass.

He could make out every single inch of her naked skin.

Her long golden locks were darkened from the water but still just as stunning. Her petite shoulders were finally loose as she relaxed. Her skin was blemished with long jagged white scars all across her body; a testament to her suffering. They only worked to further enhance her natural beauty.

James clenched his empty fist, he wished nothing more than to hurt the man responsible. How could a father do such a thing? He never would have thought to lift a single finger to his child.

James squashed the line of thought. It wasn't time for it. Right here and now, he had a magnificent woman to worship.

His eyes moved south before finally landing on her ass. Her juicy fucking ass. By the end of the night, he planned on filling it. Maybe not with his cock, but he had something else in mind.

Yara didn't even jump or flinch as he opened the shower door and stepped in behind her. Wrapping his much larger arms around her small frame. Everywhere he touched her was soft, silky, *pliable.*

"Such a good girl, waiting for me exactly where I wanted you." He nibbled on her ear as she shivered in his arms, her head falling listlessly back against his chest.

His free hand moved up to cup one of her breasts. The dichotomy between the soft skin and his rough palm sent jolts of desire directly to his balls.

He couldn't remember the last time a woman had such an effect on him.

Yara let out a musical moan, and he realized he needed to slow his bearings.

Her supple body was going to be his undoing.

"Lean over," he growled into her ear.

She did as directed. Pointing her ass into the air, her hands found the shower wall.

"A gorgeous doll."

Yara flinched as if shocked and James filed that away as a word to not use.

"Such a beautiful creature," he corrected, and the tension that had formed from his misstep left Yara immediately.

He was going to educate himself on Yara. On what made her tick. He wanted more than anything to see her unravel in his hands, on his fingers, around his cock.

He placed his free hand on her ass cheek, rubbing it gently. "We need to get you ready for my cock."

His other hand, which held the toy, moved down, his fingertips trailing against her skin as he went.

Yara hissed, "What is that?"

"Mmm just be good and let me take care of you. I know exactly what you want."

She didn't argue as he turned the toy on and moved it to her clit.

The shower's water still came down in a hot spray. It would be perfect.

With one hand reaching below and pushing the vibrator against her clit, he used his other to find the puckered rim of muscle he needed to stretch.

She couldn't see it, but the vibrator doubled as a butt plug, and he planned on pushing it into her before he fucked her tonight.

He wanted her to be filled. With the plug, his cock, and his cum.

Chapter 20

YARA

"James." His name left my lips in a breathy moan as he pushed a finger into me. Except it wasn't into my cunt. It wasn't what I expected, but I accepted the intrusion with the water acting as just enough lubricant, and the vibrator sending licks of static all the way up my spine. It was easy for him to fill me with his large rough finger.

"Marvelous. You were made for me, weren't you?"

I melted a bit under his praise. I hadn't expected to like it so much.

To *crave it*.

An older man offering his approval?

Heady. *Intoxicating*.

A drop of something I hadn't realized I needed. It did nothing to quench the vacant well of years of emptiness, but it did act as flint. And each word was a strike against the desire building.

It was propelling me to the edge even faster than his ministrations.

He gently pushed another finger in, stretching me, and I found myself pushing back onto it. Willing him to pump inside me.

"Not yet," James grunted out. "I'm getting you ready."

I started to argue, to ask him ready for what, but then he was removing the vibrator.

I rustled in annoyance.

He pulled back his fingers next and tapped me lightly on the ass. "Patience."

I felt something new.

"What is—"

He reached down spanking my cunt with his free hand. Directly on my clit. He didn't let up. Shockwaves of sensual pleasure shot across my nerves. Each smack electrified my body.

Thoroughly distracted and losing myself to this new sensation, the butt plug slid in with little resistance. He had primed me for it.

"Fuck." The word was a garbled mess that I spoke into the shower's wall.

He removed his hand from my cunt, teetering me just on the edge again.

My climax was once more just out of reach, and I wanted to turn around and hit the man.

But at the same time I was loving the delayed gratification. I felt as if I was climbing to a height I had never reached before. That each time he let up, I was only a few steps back but then had an entire mountain still to climb.

It was delicious. *Addicting*.

This man is dangerous.

Steam had long since filled the space, and the water still ran hot, bouncing off my back with stinging pebbles.

Equally, I could feel the heat of his skin, but he wasn't touching me. Just centimeters kept us separated.

I was beginning to feel self-conscious when he finally spoke.

"I want you to remember your safeword." His words echoed off the glass wall. "And if you can't speak, you tap me and I stop. You may think I am the one in control tonight, but Yara, honey, it's really you."

My toes curled in pleasure onto the rough tile below, but I didn't have time to do much more before his hands found my hips, and he grabbed me off the wall, pulling my back flat to his chest.

I hadn't seen him naked yet, but I could feel the firmness of his muscles, the scratchiness of his hair, the sturdiness of his frame.

I trusted him not to drop me, which was good because a moment later he was shutting off the shower and turning me around to lift me up onto him.

My legs reacted on their own accord stretching to encompass his hips; in doing so, I could feel every move of the plug still inside of me.

I let out a groan of appreciation as it rubbed against my inner walls.

One of his hands moved to my back while the other moved to my ass. His thumb pushed into the plug.

"That's it. That feels good, doesn't it? It's going to feel even better when my dick is pressing against it from the inside."

I opened my mouth to protest.

His hand on my back opened the shower door and then moved to my jaw, squeezing, and angling my head until I was forced to stare into his eyes.

My cunt throbbed a beat to my rapid heart that was threatening to escape the confounds of my chest.

He was touching me in ways I never thought I would like.

In ways that I didn't realize I needed.

He walked us carefully to the bedroom. "You're going to be a good girl. Now let me taste you." He sat back on the bed, pulling me with him. My knees buried into the soft sheets below, I kept my arms wrapped around his neck. The pressure he was applying on the plug didn't let up as he used his grip on my face to capture my lips.

He tugged me to him tighter as his full, soft lips moved against mine. They were wet from the shower, but I didn't care. Everything about this man was dissolving my brain power.

I was his to use. His to fuck.

But it was because I wanted him to. Because I chose this. I was safe in this moment.

This man, this *older man,* wouldn't smother me.

He wouldn't trap me. He wouldn't hurt me.

He wanted to make me feel good. It was new.

It was powerful.

His tongue pushed into my mouth, claiming mine.

He began tapping on the plug again causing jerks of pleasure to shoot across my nerves. I squirmed against him, but his grip on my jaw didn't budge.

Finally, when I grew lightheaded, he released my lips.

"You taste like honey," he murmured. His bright eyes were hooded in lust staring into my very soul.

I felt as if this man could see more than the world could.

That he was looking into my heart.

Uneasiness sparked for a moment, but before I could fall into my thoughts, he was flipping me off him and onto the mattress, catching me at the last minute.

I landed on my hands and knees on the edge of the bed.

"Just like that. Present that cunt to me. I'm going to fill it with my cum and when I'm done and you're leaking me down your thighs? I am going to clean up the mess." James' deep voice was saturated in heat.

I shivered in anticipation. He had already brought me to the edge too many times.

I needed a release.

"Please," I begged, lifting my ass up more.

"Fuck." I heard shuffling and then the sound of a vibrator. "Hold this to your clit, I need both hands," he directed, using one hand to place the toy, finding the right spot immediately.

I used one hand to keep my face off the mattress and the other found the toy. "James," I groaned out. I was nearing my release again.

"Just like that." His large, calloused hands found my hips.

He lined up.

And he plunged all the way in; his thick cock stretching me to my limits. I could feel him pushing against the butt plug, and combined with the vibrator, it only added to the buildup of before.

I came unexpectedly, and an uninhibited scream fell from my lips in surprise. "James!" His name left me in a raspy sob.

"That's it. You're taking my cock so perfectly. You were made for me. Let me fill you up. Let me test your limits."

I was still pulsating around him as he began to pull all the way out and slam back in, it was only his sturdy hands on my hips keeping me in place.

"Fuck you're taking all of me," he rasped out before he began to push a rhythm into me. It was all I could do to keep the vibrator in place, but I didn't want to drop it.

Didn't want to disappoint him.

I *needed* his approval.

"That's it, just like that. Fuck, Yara. You're so small. How are you taking me like this?"

I whimpered as he sped up his pace, but even still as he skirted the line of pain, I was feeling pleasure more than anything else.

This is everything I didn't know I needed.

The thought was a mantra that repeated in my head every so often. It kept my self-consciousness at bay, never allowing it to ruin this moment.

He thrust once more, hitting a spot even deeper than before and let out a guttural noise.

He went still, buried fully inside as he filled me.

I expected him to pull out right away, but he didn't.

"Fuck, feed that greedy cunt. Fill you with my cum. Tell me what you want."

"I want you to fill me." I finally dropped the vibrator and used both hands on the mattress to push myself further onto him.

"Fuck! Yara!" He yanked me by hips off of him, flipping me over, and slamming back into me.

His bright striking eyes met mine. They were swirling with hunger.

Intensity.

Adoration.

He leaned over me, his hands landing on either side of my head.

I clenched around his length.

"Don't fucking start with me, little girl." His face darkened. This wasn't the businessman I met at dinner.

This was a predator that had finally escaped his cage.

He leaned down licking up the column of my neck, sucking gently on the skin there. He hummed against my skin, and I squirmed underneath him.

He lightly thrust into me as his mouth explored my neck. After a few more minutes I couldn't help the moans that were leaving me, he was working me towards the edge again, keeping me on a tight line of just teetering onto what I needed. But he wasn't letting me fall off.

"I think it's time to clean you again." His breath tickled my ear.

He finally pulled free from me, but a moment later, he was returning.

His eyes met mine as he pushed something into my cunt.

"Need to plug you up so none of my cum can trickle down your thighs while I clean you. Wouldn't want you wasting it."

He reached one firm hand a bit lower, his other finding my clit and rubbing it. I felt a bit of pressure as he removed the butt plug.

He left for a moment, and I heard the water running before he returned. "Come on, let's get you cleaned up before our next round."

Chapter 21

MATEO

This stupid fucking tracker doesn't work to find a pinpoint? 300 feet range? How the fuck is that going to help when she's in a god damn hotel?

Mateo was furious, raging, vibrating with unused energy.

I'm safe. I'll call in the morning.

Yara's text bounced around his mind for the hundredth time.

Emilio had gotten into her work computer earlier only to find the discretion date tonight wasn't even on the schedule. The man she was on a date with, that she had disappeared with. Wasn't. Even. Vetted.

They didn't even know his name.

Mateo turned to Kazi. "You're lucky she likes you."

Mateo watched Kazi roll his shoulders back and side eye the front desk attendant.

The idiot attendant had been watching them warily ever since Mateo threatened their life.

The worker deserved it. How could they not remember his little bee? She was indistinguishable.

Much to Mateo's chagrin, Kazi didn't even appear worried. He had expressed that she most likely had wanted to ditch them, especially after Izzy's distraction call. Mateo didn't agree.

"She's okay. She'll call us in the morning."

Mateo turned on Kazi. "She is FUCKING some STRANGE MAN! She has a fucking stalker, *pendejo*!" he roared into Kazi's face, wanting nothing more than to pulverize the man.

He wouldn't. If only for Yara.

Yara had buried so deep into Mateo that he wasn't quite sure when or how it happened.

But he knew one thing for certain, what had started with a mere curiosity had led to a full out obsession.

Kazi appeared to accept Mateo's anger, offering a reassuring smile to the hotel employees. "Yes, I am upset too. But I also know better than to draw attention to myself."

"Yeah, so little attention. She doesn't even know you want her. Fucking idiot." Mateo was pissed. He was throwing punches.

He needed another Liam. A distraction.

He hadn't realized how useless the tracker would be.

Kazi hummed an obnoxious noise, grating further on Mateo's nerves.

"Who owns the company?" Mateo spat out.

"What company?" Kazi replied, leaning against a white pillar in the hotel's lobby.

Relaxing.

It took everything for Mateo not to swing at Kazi.

"The tracking device company. I want the CEO. His personal address. I'm calling Emilio back." Mateo clenched his fists. He needed to relieve some of his... frustrations.

Chapter 22

YARA

James swiped his rough fingers up and down my body in the shower. He had already thoroughly cleaned me, and it had done nothing to calm my nerves.

One hand reached down to my clit, pinching it lightly. I clenched around the plug letting out a breathy moan.

"You are perfection." His voice was saturated in emotion.

I shifted, looking up into his eyes. This man was affecting me more than I cared to admit. I had planned for this to be a one time thing, at least with him, but now I wasn't so sure.

I was melting with every word he spoke, with every touch.

He was filling some hidden part of my soul that had been lacking for too long.

It was almost terrifying how much I wanted this man to stick around. To become a permanent fixture in my life.

But how would that even work? My feelings for Kazi had not diminished, and furthermore, Mateo was slowly carving his way into my heart.

James's fingers traced the line of one particularly nasty scar up my stomach, digging into the flesh, pulling me out of my inner turmoil.

Of wondering what was wrong or right.

His face darkened as he focused on the blemish, but then his lips curled. "Get me ready to stuff you again, will you, honey?" His guttural voice sent shockwaves across my skin.

Usually, I didn't like to be directed with what to do. I liked to be the one in control, but the way he spoke? His voice?

I dropped carefully to my knees in the shower, enjoying the roughness of the tile, and the way the position squeezed the plug in my cunt.

My hand reached out to his impressive cock. I could see now why he hadn't expected it to fit. I'm not quite sure how it did.

Or how I would be stuffing it into my mouth.

Separating my lips, I took in his velvet tip and swirled my tongue.

"That's so good, show me how much you want me to fuck you again." His hand wrapped into my wet hair, but he didn't force his way further. Instead, he held me gently, allowing me to go at my own pace.

I opened my mouth a bit more, slowly moving my head forward and forcing him to the very back of my throat.

He groaned in appreciation and it sent desire shooting directly to my throbbing core.

I swallowed around him at the very back of my throat, using my hand to wrap around the remainder that wouldn't fit.

Hollowing my cheeks, I began to experiment, using his noises as guidance. I found he particularly liked it when I tongued his tip before pushing him aggressively down my throat.

After repeating a few times, he let out a particularly loud groan.

"Fuck, no more." In an impressive move, he used his hand in my hair to pull me off his cock and his other to bring me to my feet.

Letting go of my hair, he reached between us.

"Yara," he growled the word, gently gliding the plug out of my cunt. Before any of his cum could escape, he was lifting me and filling me with his cock.

"James," I gasped out, wrapping my legs around him and burying my head into his neck.

Somehow this was different from just earlier tonight. I was more comfortable.

If after less than one night I was already this familiar with him? This trusting?

How long will it take for him to get close enough to ruin me?

"*Fuck*, I've got you." He turned the shower off and walked us back to the bedroom, dripping water with every step.

This moment was reminiscent of how our night began, but this time when he sat back on the bed, his cock was fully buried inside.

Sitting on him caused it to push even further in. Stretching me past the point of before.

"Fuck!" I screamed the word out, leaning back and shutting my eyes in bliss as he began to pump into me from below, his large hand coming up to pinch and rub on my clit.

"So beautiful. Such a good girl taking this cock. Letting it stretch you. Put your hands on my shoulders—hold on tight."

That was the only warning I got before he began to thrust hard beats up into me. My fingernails digging into his skin, leaving crescent marks in their wake.

For just a moment, it was like I was riding a fucking bull before his free hand caught me on the waist and held me in place.

Everything was overwhelming, the sensations, the heat of his skin, the fullness, the connection.

In the chaos of our bodies movement, his eyes met mine, they swirled with pure unadulterated *devotion*.

The dam exploded, my body convulsing around him.

He slowed his movements, his hands coming up to cup my face, his lips pressing to mine. I swirled my hips on him as his tongue invaded my mouth, and he groaned, intensifying the kiss.

Only a moment later, I felt it as he came inside me. Again. I was thoroughly wet and mostly ruined at this point.

I pulled back from his lips and squirmed to get up, but he didn't let me.

"Stay like this for a bit?" he asked, shifting us up on the mattress.

I acquiesced, allowing him to manhandle me and resting against him, my face burrowing into his scratchy chest.

Relaxing into a post sex haze.

After a bit, the heat of our moment slowly faded and the realization of what we had done turned my cheeks pink.

I shifted a bit trying to escape again, but before I could, he caught my chin with his hand, forcing me to look him into his eyes.

His eerily familiar eyes.

"You know I don't want this to be a one-time thing," James murmured, watching me carefully.

"I thought I was too young for you?" I reached between us, jabbing him lightly in his chest. But I had already decided to continue down this path. I wouldn't ghost him like I did every other man I crawled into bed with.

Well except Kazi. And technically Mateo.

"You are," he chuckled softly.

I rolled my hips, and his cock jumped inside my cunt. I could feel his liquid slowly dripping down but ignored it.

"Minx." He smiled up at me, crows feet forming as his face lit up. "I want to fall asleep like this, but I don't know if we would get any rest that way." He pushed my damp hair behind my ears, leaning forward he pressed a kiss to my forehead. "Go clean up without me, get dressed, and then come back. I want to hold you while we sleep tonight." His voice was incredibly tender.

I didn't even think to argue.

Chapter 23

J.W.

James watched Yara dress, his eyes never leaving her. They were both finally clean and while he wanted nothing more than to fall asleep against her naked body, he knew she needed sleep.

Just as he did.

And there would always be next time. Because he was determined at this point for Yara to take up a permanent residence in his life. He just hoped she felt the same.

He lifted the sheets for her to slide in next to him.

She carefully settled onto the bed, and he tugged her back against his chest.

He marinated for a moment in her warmth. He had been alone for too long.

"So, what is your story?" Yara mumbled softly, shifting closer to him.

He pressed a kiss into the back of her hair, clenching his arms around her much smaller body.

"You gave me your truth earlier? Well I will do the same. I was never married, but I had somebody for a long time. She was practically my wife. We were together for almost fifteen years and while I had tried to tie the knot several times, she never seemed interested." James let out a whoosh of air.

He was grateful he didn't have to watch Yara's face. He didn't want to see the typical judgment he was used to witnessing.

"We shared a child and after fifteen years together, they both disappeared without a trace." James's voice cracked. He had looked everywhere for the both of them, but their names weren't anywhere. There was no paper trail. It was as if they had disappeared without a trace.

"They disappeared?" Yara whispered out hoarsely into the mattress.

"I came home from a business trip and they were both gone," James confirmed, his words muffled by Yara's hair.

"Your child, what was her name?"

Had he said he had a daughter? Or was it that obvious? "Isobella, but we always called her Izzy." James was so wrapped up in his own grief, his own shortcomings, his own memories that he didn't realize Yara had stiffened in his arms.

Didn't realize that she was no longer resting comfortably against him.

Didn't realize that he was holding his daughter's best friend.

Chapter 24

KAZI

Kazi was still leaning against a pillar in the hotel when his phone began to ring. He cast a glance around looking for Mateo. The man was still off somewhere letting off some steam.

He pulled the phone out.

Yara.

Fucking finally.

Answering it, he didn't even have time to get a word in.

"I fucked up," Yara whispered softly into the phone.

It was nearing 4AM.

What has happened? Is she okay?

He knew better than to hammer her with questions, so he remained silent willing her to continue.

"I'm coming down to the lobby. We need to leave. I need to call Izzy."

Kazi could hear the panic in her voice, but he kept his cool. "I'm here. I'll have a car ready. We can't go to our apartment because there was a bed bug outbreak. I found a replacement." He decided it was best to rip that bandage off now. While the clean up crew had done what was needed to cover up Mateo's indiscretions, their bed still needed to be fully replaced.

And the smell of bleach?

That wouldn't dissipate too soon either.

Yara was so wrapped up in whatever was going on she didn't even question him. "Okay, I'm getting in the elevator."

The call cut off.

Kazi finally moved from his position where he had stayed stock-still for the last several hours. The employees here watched him with suspicious eyes, but he ignored it. He confirmed the car was still ready and marched his way to the elevator.

He couldn't keep playing this game with Yara.

Mateo might be ridiculous, but he was also right.

Kazi wasn't making any headway in his passive approach.

Kazi knew what she had done. He had been worried she would for years, but he thought he had more time. Thought the stalker would keep her from following through.

The elevator opened to Yara. A hickey shined on her neck, her hair was a disheveled mess, and she was wearing a practically see-through dress.

He quickly shed his jacket, wrapping it around her shoulders, before lifting her bridal style.

"I fucked up." Yara didn't fight him, instead her arms wrapped around his neck as he walked them through the lobby.

"Are you okay?" Kazi's blood was pounding through his veins.

He wasn't opposed to murder if a man had hurt his Yara.

His Yara.

Yara's bright eyes found his, they were glassy. "I made a mistake. I met with a man. I didn't use our typical background process. I thought I had it handled, but Kazi–" She let out a sob as he finally made it out of the hotel.

Kazi felt the weight of eyes on the back of his head, but he ignored it, sliding into the waiting car and pulling Yara gently with him. Keeping her in his lap.

She wouldn't be leaving his sight again for the foreseeable future.

"What happened?" Kazi's voice was gruff. "What did you do Miss Yara?"

She pushed her face into the crook of his neck, breathing him in and out. "I met a man. I had a wonderful night, but Kazi..." Yara sniffled. "He's... he's..."

He grabbed Yara's shoulders, shaking her. "Fuck, Yara. Spit it out! You're scaring me!"

He saw the driver shift, and he clocked that he didn't recognize the man. It wasn't their typical driver. Before he could follow down that line of thought, Yara distracted him entirely.

She leaned forward until her lips were touching his ear. "It was Izzy's dad. Her *dead* dad."

Kazi dropped his hold on Yara, falling back into the seat.

Fuck. Fuck. *Fuck!*

All thoughts of the driver were extinguished. He couldn't tell Emilio. "Does he know?"

Yara shifted over into her own seat, leaning against Kazi. "Know that he just fucked his long-lost daughter's best friend? Filled her with his cum?" She laughed caustically.

Kazi's fists clenched in jealousy. He willed himself to calm down; he couldn't lose his cool, he needed to be here for Yara.

"No, I ran away like the coward I am. And besides that, I don't believe in coincidences, how did he find me? End up in my radar?"

Yara's words echoed around Kazi's mind, but he didn't have too long to process them.

"Why are we where Mateo's been staying?" Yara's voice was saturated in uneasiness.

Kazi shifted his attention out the window to the fortress Mateo decided to rent when he heard of Yara's stalker. Where he had attempted to force them both to move to.

The driver made it through the gated entrance before the man of the hour made his appearance.

"Why is Mateo covered in blood?"

Sure enough, the psychopath himself was walking towards the car. Knife in one hand, blood covering the other. Mateo had been blood-free in the hotel after his run in with Liam, while they searched for Yara. The clean up team had already been dispatched to cover up his first mess.

Apparently Mateo had no qualms with leaving a trail of destruction all over this city.

Perhaps Kazi should have called first, but he hadn't known Mateo was actually going to go after the CEO of the tracking company.

Kazi would just have to call the *family* again to sort through all of this.

Fuck.

Chapter 25

YARA

I didn't wait for Kazi's response, hopping out of the car instead.

For a sick moment, I thought Mateo might use the knife on me. Instead, he threw it to the ground, leaned forward, and wrapped me in his large bulky arms.

"Mi pequeña abeja, where the fuck have you been?" he growled. "A hickey? You let this man mark you? Who is he?"

"Where did the blood come from?" I raised an eyebrow taking in the rest of Mateo's appearance.

He had clearly been in the middle of... something.

"Touche." His gruff voice sent shockwaves to my toes.

In this moment, I was clearly a crazy person.

Let's see–I started the night by fucking a man twice my age, doing all sorts of nasty with him only to find out he was in fact, my best friend's dad.

I then allowed Kazi to take me to an undisclosed location while he manhandled me in the car. *Did I mention how much I had enjoyed that?*

And now here I was in Mateo's arms, the blood from his hand staining my skin whilst his gruff voice sent shockwaves to my sore cunt.

Perhaps my therapist was right. I should take medication. Maybe the years of abuse were affecting me more than I realized.

"Want to explain why I'm here and not at my apartment?"

Mateo shifted my body until his hands found the curve of my ass, lifting me until I was made to wrap my legs around his frame.

"I took out the trash there, it caused a mess." His thumb covered where I knew a hickey to be, pressing into the skin there.

"So not bed bugs?" I eyed Kazi speculatively who had now joined us as Mateo marched up to the front door.

Twisting around, I found it was a metal padlocked iron door.

I let out an exasperated sigh. "Just take me to a spare room, and I need some clothes please." I didn't have the mental capacity to unwrap anything right now. It was nearing 5AM, and I was exhausted.

I needed some sleep, and then I needed to call Izzy.

Chapter 26

D

D's precious angel had finally taken a misstep. Yara had kept D from her home for so long, but he had caught a break.

He hadn't expected this to work. But here they were, in his car. Letting him chauffeur them to her home.

He was irritated to see the security measures, but he could work around that.

D considered for a moment just taking them both and driving off, but he didn't want to deal with the man. *Kazi*.

He saw her new acquaintance step out of the house. The blood and knife were mildly startling, but he expected nothing less from the oaf.

When they were both out of the car, he snapped a few pictures already planning his next letter, except maybe it was time to try something new...

He was running out of patience. If she didn't answer him soon?

Well, he would be forced to take action.

And now he knew exactly how to get to her.

Chapter 27

YARA

"Go away!" I shouted through the door for the thousandth time.

I had been working from this room for the last three weeks, and I had barely left it other than to eat.

Three weeks of hiding away and not acknowledging the shit storm I was in the midst of.

I had delegated all tasks as necessary to our team and was doing the bare minimum for work.

I was still at Mateo's "house."

It was nicer on the inside than I had expected. The spare room he had given me came equipped with a bathroom and Kazi had been kind enough to stock me up with clothes.

Both of the men checked on me often, but I had decided I needed time to figure out what the fuck I was going to do. And I was self-aware enough to admit that I was a chicken shit and didn't want to deal with my expanding feelings for the three men that had taken my life by storm.

Kazi, Mateo, James.

James. I had dreamed every night of his hands on my body, of the way he made me feel.

Of the fact that he was my best friend's dad.

I was trying to gain the courage to call Izzy to let her know who I found. What I had done.

For the millionth time, I reached for my phone to call her.

What exactly would I say?

Hey, you know how your mom told you your dad was dead? How she kept you from the funeral? How she changed your last name? How she moved you across the country? How she met your step-dad and skipped off into the sunset?

Well, you know how weird we thought that was? Ha ha ha. Turns out your mom is a psycho bitch, and your dad is alive.

Oh, and I fucked him. A lot. And it might have been the best sex of my life. Just call me mommy, I'll be better than yours, promise.

Izzy was an amazing friend, but even she wouldn't be okay with this.

My phone's vibrating pulled me out of my internal dialogue. I expected to see James calling...again.

But it was actually Izzy.

Trepidation sunk into my gut.

Fuck, fuck, *fuck*!

"Yara?" the quiet voice came from the phone.

Apparently in my turmoil I had accidentally answered.

"What's up girl?" I put on my best bravado and cheery voice, pulling the phone up to my ear.

"I caught Harry." Harry—her current bad decision, her *boyfriend*. Izzy's voice was monotone, matter of fact. "He was dick deep in Hallie's asshole. I have a video of it."

"Hallie?" My own anxiety was replaced with outrage. "Your fucking step-sister? What the actual fuck? What did he have to say for himself?"

She snorted sarcastically. "That I made the video with AI. I met him out—"

I grumbled into the phone.

"In public!" she reassured before sighing heavily. "I'm just too chunky, nobody is ever going to love me. I'm always going to be stuck in this endless cycle of vanilla men."

My heart went out to her. Izzy was one of the most beautiful people I had ever met. Inside and out, but she didn't see it for herself. Not that you could ever tell; she was the queen at faux confidence. "Stop with that self-deprecating bullshit. We both know that man wasn't shit," I huffed out. I may have my own personal issues with my body image, and maybe it was hypocritical, but I knew Izzy had the ability to love herself, she just needed a little push sometimes.

"Yeah… and we have our fucking reunion coming up. Just about a month now."

In my own distress, I had forgotten about that entirely.

That's when I would tell her. It would be better in person.

Or maybe I really *was* just a chicken shit.

Either or, really.

"I think it's about time I use your dating site too." Izzy chuckled uneasily.

Ice perforated my veins, memories of James popping up behind my eyelids. Even after weeks, I couldn't get the thought of him out of my mind. Of how he made me feel. Of how, even in spite of the knowledge that he was Izzy's dad, I still wanted him. *Needed* him.

That he had started to fix something I never realized was broken. His words were a thread and now here I was a half sewed up mess.

I needed to make sure. To be certain. Maybe it *was* a coincidence and I could sing kumbaya into the sunset with James. "Ooh if only our families could see us now, dating site extraordinaires. I know your mother would bust a gasket, but I wonder how your dad would have felt. What was your dad's name again?" Fuck that sounded stupid even to my own ears. I was not slick at *all*.

She went silent for a few moments, and I was almost afraid I had crossed some invisible line, but then she eventually spoke, her voice lighter than I expected. "Yeah, I don't really talk about him too much. James Wright was his name. Why?"

Well, that answered that. The last piece of hope I held onto crumbled. "Just curious." I hummed. "Love you Izzy, you know that right?"

"You're not dying from some incurable disease are you?" Izzy joked.

"Funny, look remember Harry wasn't shit. Let me know if you need me to 'take care of him.'"

"Who's got jokes now? Well Maddox is here to take me home. Got to go, talk soon." Izzy ended the call, and I let the phone drop to the ground.

"When are you going to tell her?"

I jumped about twenty feet into the air. "Kazi," I hissed out. I hadn't seen him sneak into my room, but here he was, laying across the mattress.

Mateo right next to him.

"Both of you? Really?" I cocked an arm on my hip in frustration. Here they were again, pushing my boundaries.

"We missed you. What can we say?" Mateo stretched out across the mattress knocking into Kazi aggressively.

"You're both liars," I bit the words out. Sure I was staying with them now, but I wasn't an idiot. They both had been acting up.

Kazi and Mateo weren't cousins. My house didn't have bed bugs. The scars that Mateo carried told a story I wasn't sure I was ready to hear. The blood that he had on him when I showed up here was suspicious as fuck.

His job as a bodyguard? I could smell the bullshit.

I had buried my head in the sand for the last several weeks because in simple terms: I wanted to. But now? Here with them both, I wanted answers.

If I couldn't get to the bottom of James, I planned on at least getting answers from them.

"Mateo, what do you do for a living?" I asked.

"I told you he's—"

I cut Kazi off. "I'm asking Mateo."

Mateo stood up, cracking his neck. He took menacing steps towards me. His face darkening, his mahogany eyes swirling in promise.

"Oh, is that how it's going to be?"

He was so close to me now I had to crane my neck upwards to meet his eyes, his woodsy scent enveloping me. He reached a hand up grabbing my chin, pinching it tightly between two strong rough fingers. "I'm your worst nightmare."

Whatever he expected it wasn't for me to rip away from him and die from a laughing fit. Hands on my knees I gasped out, "Does that usually work?"

He apparently didn't like my reaction because next I knew I was being thrown onto the bed; I landed next to Kazi. "I finally dug into your database. Found your forms. Discovered what you wanted, your safeword. The man." Mateo was snarling as he stepped to the bed.

"Mateo," Kazi chastised in warning.

"She wants this. She wants the danger. She wants the rush of being out of control." Mateo's words caused licks of unexpected desire to roll across my skin.

What the fuck is happening?

"I don't understand what's happening."

Literally. The whiplash was real.

"I'm finishing what I started with you. It's been almost an entire month. I let you get comfortable in my presence, but now it's time for me to collect. I know your safeword, but Yara, I think you'll be brave enough to not use it."

Mateo began to strip his clothes, first his shirt leaving an impressive spread of skin that rolled across a strong chest and rippled abs.

Even more prevalent–the scars. They lined every inch of his skin, and I did my best not to react to the sight of them. I had seen them once before in the hotel room but taking them in from a distance was different.

They told a story.

"Mateo," Kazi's voice pitched with an unknown emotion, and I turned to him to see if he could explain to me when we had landed in the twilight zone.

"You gonna take that tail out from between your legs and claim this beautiful woman? Or are you going to hide your feelings and die in friend-zone hell."

My confusion was sky-rocketing. I rolled to face Kazi entirely.

"Kazi?" I asked softly.

He reached up, pushing his dark hair from his eyes. "I love you, you know that right?"

"I do." I loved him, too. He was my lifeline in this otherwise desolate city. He was the calm I needed to wage war against the night terrors that plagued me. He was the anchor that kept me from being swept away in the chaos of my life.

"Well, you stupid ignorant woman. I am in love with you. I have been for years. How could I not be? Even if you worry me to death, and are always saturated in chaos, I wouldn't have it any other way. One day when the time is right, I have a secret I need to tell you, but I am going to promise you one thing. You can trust me, I would never do anything to hurt you."

I didn't have time to truly process all of his words, but what I saw when our eyes met, spoke volumes. I watched a reel of all the years of concern, care, and protection Kazi provided me. It struck me in that moment exactly what Kazi had been showing me in his actions. In his attentiveness. In his constant companionship. In his willingness to adjust his entire life on my behalf. For my sake.

He loves me. He is in love with me.

Just as the realization washed over me, Kazi's lips crashed into mine, as if all at once, his claim on me, my eyes, my lips, my *heart* was finally made.

His body covered my frame, his hair tickling my nose.

He pulled back, watching me carefully. "Scuttlebutt," he stated my safeword before leaning slowly, carefully down.

Even in this moment he was making sure I knew he was safe. That he wouldn't push me or hurt me.

With Kazi I didn't need paperwork binding my safety. I trusted his words. I knew inherently that if I needed to escape, for this to stop, he would. No questions asked.

His lips pressed against me again, capturing mine. Stealing my breath, my heart, my *soul*. Kazi represented all things good in my life. He was the reason I thrived for so many years.

His tongue lashed out, pushing against my teeth, I opened for him.

Kazi was safety, warmth, protection. For a long time I thought it was odd how he pushed himself into my life, how he would never let me out of his sight, how he immediately moved in when I mentioned it as a joke.

But now? Here in this moment? *I don't fucking care.*

When every flag in your life is red, you have to look for the lightest shade.

He separated from me again, taking my breath with him. One of his hands moved to cup my cheek, the other buried into the mattress below. "Miss Yara, I'm not leaving your side. Whether you want me to or not, so please *jagiya*, make sure this is what you want. I won't push you, but once we cross this line? I won't stop."

My heart beat against my chest in painful thuds; I should be feeling anxious, overwhelmed, apprehensive.

But I didn't. All I felt was excitement.

I had wanted Kazi for years, but I didn't want to lose him. Didn't want to cross a line for him to turn me down. "You promise to tell me your secrets?"

"One at a time." Kazi's smile encompassed his face, his eyes lit up as he leaned back and looked over his shoulder.

"It's not just him. You're going to have to handle us both. Because from here on out? We're a package deal, little bee." Mateo's guttural voice filled the room.

I wanted to be upset, to argue. But even in this brief period? Even with our minimal interactions? Mateo had dug his way under my skin.

He was someone that I could tell was dangerous. And maybe it was the trauma that had formed inside at such a young age, but being around danger when you know it isn't going to hurt you?

It was a heady feeling. An adrenaline rush.

"Fuck." The word left my lips raspily as I laid back on the bed, watching Kazi's face carefully. "You'll both take care of me? Make me feel good?"

Why am I giving in so easily to this?

Why does it feel like this is such a long time coming?

Kazi's lips curled; his russet eyes brightened in promise.

"Yes, come here." Mateo pushed Kazi off of me, tugging me up onto his lap, forcing me to straddle him. He smirked. "First secret?" His hand found my arm where a scar had formed from the night of our first encounter. "This is a tracker. Your birth control is gone."

It took a few moments to process exactly what he said, it was so out of left field. My mind flashed back to the memory of the mysterious gash on my arm that I had no recollection of causing. "What the actual–" I couldn't even finish the thought as I hissed the words trying to pull back from him.

Except why wasn't I feeling any anxiety? Why had the confession caused desire to shoot directly to my core?

What is wrong with me?

Was I just as broken as I had thought? Had the years of abuse actually torn me apart, and I was just a ticking bomb just waiting to go off?

He held onto my arm with his sturdy grip, his long rough fingers wrapping around it. "I did it. Don't want to lose you now that I've found you." Mateo's eyes churned in promise. "Except the damn thing doesn't work well, I'll need to get you an upgrade, wouldn't want you slipping off again."

I shut my eyes, breathing in and out slowly. The feminist in me wanted to fight Mateo, tell him he had no right, that it was my fucking body.

But why was said body coiled in anticipation, why did I want more of this crazy man, why did I melt under his attention? "You don't even fucking know me." I finally let out.

"Don't I?" He let go of my arm to find my wrist.

My eyes flashed open. "No, you don't. Let me go."

"Mateo." Kazi was lying next to us, watching our interaction guardedly.

"I know you're stronger than you think. I know you're going to let Kazi and I fuck you. I know you're going to accept that I'm not going anywhere, that I am just as damaged as you are. And I know you are going to love every fucking piece of me, just as I love you. Inside and out." He tugged my wrist up to his mouth.

I watched in frozen shock as he brought his lips to my wrist, and before I could yank back, his teeth met the flesh there, he bit down over the scars, sucking onto the flesh. I anticipated it hurting. It didn't.

It felt... *good.*

Kazi reached over and I expected him to stop this, but to my surprise, he took my other wrist and mimicked Mateo, biting down over the scars there.

I let out an uninhibited moan as new emotions were swept up into the cause of my scars.

Enjoyable memories, ones I could look back on happily.

"Okay," the word whooshed out.

It was all either of them needed.

Chapter 28

KAZI

"This is how it's going to go. I'm going to fuck you, fill that pussy with my cum and then when I'm ready to? I'm going to fill that ass up too," Mateo grumbled at Yara.

Kazi watched her warily. Sure he had read through what she had allowed the other man, James, to do to her. But that was because she told him it was what she wanted.

Kazi imagined the same wouldn't occur here. But he was happy to sit back and watch them duke it out. He already knew what he planned to do with Yara.

Smack!

Yara's hand landed against Mateo's arm. "No, that very much *isn't* going to happen. You just said you removed my birth control, you ridiculous man!"

Kazi chuckled to himself as Mateo snarled. Kazi was no longer worried about the man with Yara. He could recognize Mateo's infatuation, his growing *love*. And while Kazi didn't ever expect to be in this predicament, he wasn't sure if he would have been enough for Yara.

Over the years, he had barely been enough for himself.

Yara had been the one who brought light into an otherwise dull life.

"You let the other man fill you with his cum! I need to saturate you in mine! Make his run for the fucking hills."

"Ew! What does that even mean?! If you had read the file, you would have seen he had a vasectomy!" Yara was pounding on Mateo's chest now as she screamed in his face.

It was hot watching her lose her cool. Especially when Kazi wasn't involved.

"They aren't one hundred percent effective." Mateo's stern baritone voice rolled into the room.

Yara stopped pounding on him for a moment. In one quick move, she spun out of Mateo's lap into Kazi's waiting arms.

He wrapped them around her tightly, relaxing in her familiarity. It had been weeks since he had held her like this.

After years of sleeping side by side, it had hurt him in a way he hadn't expected.

He wasn't used to being lonely. Not since she had fallen like a cannonball into his life.

He couldn't go another moment without her.

He had realized it years ago, she would never be escaping him, but now he needed to press that into her.

He nuzzled against Yara's neck, and she let out a lyrical giggle. He whispered into the column of her throat. "How about this, I fuck you"–she squirmed a bit as he pushed his dick into her ass–"with a condom. And maybe if you're feeling generous you can show Mateo what that sharp mouth of yours can do?" He worded it as a suggestion, but he wasn't quite sure what he would do if she said no.

Yara hummed in agreement, wiggling purposefully against his dick. Hardening it past the point of comfort.

Mateo watched them both with calculating eyes before a sinister smile formed eerily across his face.

Kazi ignored it, he needed to be inside Yara. To finally establish the connection that had grown between them over the years.

"Kazi."

Her breathy voice was his undoing. He reached between them, taking down his shorts as Mateo tugged hers off.

Kazi's hands found the soft smooth skin of her unblemished ass, and he stroked it. "Do you want me to worship this now or later, Miss Yara?"

"It's Yara. Just Yara."

Kazi chuckled, how should he explain to her the nuances of why he called her miss? Another time.

"Fuck, this is hot just to watch. Pull her shirt up just over her tits," Mateo commanded.

Kazi was a bit irritated at the idiot's demands, but he agreed with the sentiment. However, before he could reach to acquiesce, Yara shimmied out of it entirely, throwing it at Mateo's face.

Kazi stuttered for a moment.

Does Yara realize how many men Mateo would have killed over less than that?

Mateo chuckled. "Is that right? Are you going to be a brat, little bee?"

"Lick my cunt, get me ready for Kazi to fuck me and maybe I won't be."

Kazi nuzzled into Yara's neck, snickering lightly as Mateo let loose a full belly laugh.

"As the brat commands."

Kazi decided to help. "Trust me?" he whispered the words into her ear, enjoying the way she shivered against him.

He wanted nothing more than to push his dick deep inside her, but he was a patient man, he could wait a little longer.

"I shouldn't, but I do." Emotion seeped into her words.

"We know your safeword. Please use it, *jagiya*, if you need to. And if you can't say it, two taps to my palm and we'll stop." Kazi lifted one of her legs up to allow Mateo the access he needed.

He expected to feel jealousy, possessiveness, but as Mateo's head moved to the space between her thighs, Kazi found it was only adding to his own desire.

Kazi watched as Mateo viciously attacked her.

It was animalistic, the way he was ravaging her thighs, licking, and sucking, two of his long fingers hooking into her. Yara's breathing turned unsteady, the movement brought Kazi's attention to her chest. His free hand came up to stroke the porcelain soft skin there, pinching her pebbled nipple between his fingers. He would be content to lay like this for hours, exploring her body, how she reacted to his touch.

"Kazi," she breathed.

He had never heard his name whispered in such a loving manner before. The fervent gasp pushing him closer to a breaking point. He was unsure what would happen when he hit it.

"Oh is that right brat?" Mateo's tone was humorously annoyed. In Kazi's periphery, Mateo's face shifted up and Kazi saw a flash of teeth.

"*Be gentle.*" The words slipped from his lips in concern.

To Kazi, it looked painful, but Yara's sounds told another story. Her back arching off of the bed in pleasure, her breast filling into his hand, her moans vibrating against his skin.

After a few moments, Mateo came up for air. "Get ready to fuck her, she's almost there. I want to watch her come around your cock."

Yara grumbled, reaching for Mateo's head to pull him back where she wanted him.

"Yes I know, I know you needy brat."

Kazi carefully, using his free hand, reached behind him and opened the nightstand drawer, pulling out the box of condoms he had put there.

His day job was as her assistant and that meant to make sure she was always ready for anything.

Including him.

Without further ado, he ripped the package with his teeth, reaching between them to roll it down his dick.

"Now," Mateo roared.

It was difficult to push into her from behind, both of them lying on their sides.

"Fucking aim better!"

Kazi wasn't sure how he felt about Mateo guiding his dick into her, but then he couldn't focus on anything else.

He pushed all the way in, pulling her flush to him, gripping onto her skin tightly.

She screamed in bliss, tightening on his dick.

Fuck!

It was everything he could do to not lose himself to it. To be a two pump chump.

With his hold on Yara, he gestured at the bed to Mateo and was grateful when the idiot moved as he wanted.

He needed better leverage.

In a careful motion, he pulled out of Yara for just a moment to reposition them.

He had her on her hands and knees now.

"Kazi, what are you—?"

He slammed back into her, one hand on her hip bone, the other finding her clit, rubbing circles there.

"That's it, look at you taking his cock in that pussy of yours. Do you like that? Or do you want to keep being a brat?" Mateo repositioned until he was in front of her on his knees. "You going to suck down this cock while he fucks you from behind? Or do you want me to shove it in that tight ass of yours?"

Kazi raised an eyebrow at Mateo before refocusing his attention on Yara. On the way his dick slid in and out of her.

How she was suffocating him.

How she was opening her mouth for Mateo, sucking him down while Kazi filled her from behind.

Kazi pinched her clit hard and she tightened around him again.

The static that had slowly built deep in his gut licked up and down his spine, electricity zapping him as he came.

It was ethereal, and for a moment, he didn't realize he had stopped breathing. After the lack of oxygen hit him, he gulped in a few breaths.

Even with the condom, he wanted nothing more than to stay there. Keep his dick inside her. Claim her as his own.

This would *not* be the last time.

"That's it. Choke on it. Look at those tears falling. Now I'm going to cum and you're going to swallow it."

Kazi stayed inside, but bent over her, moving his hand to one of hers.

Showing her that she could tap him, that he would stop this if she wanted.

She didn't.

Even as Mateo forced his way down her throat, as he felt her gag, as tears streamed down her face.

"What a good little bee. Now swallow every drop," Mateo commanded her before a moment later, he fell back on the bed and Yara took in several deep breaths of air.

Kazi gently and carefully pulled free from her, but he didn't let her go.

"Take the condom off, my hands are full," he told Mateo, carefully arranging Yara into his arms.

"You're lucky she likes you," Mateo grumbled, removing the offending plastic.

Kazi didn't deign to respond. "We'll be back. Let us have this."

Mateo didn't even argue. He tossed the used plastic in the trash before leaning back on the bed. "Hurry up. I have a brat's ass to fill."

Chapter 29

YARA

My body was vibrating as Kazi carried me into the bathroom; he set me gently onto the ground.

"Do your business, I'll be back in a moment." He leaned over, turning the shower on before stepping outside the door. I could hear as he leaned against it.

It sounded like he and Mateo were whispering in hushed tones, but I couldn't make out the words.

I turned to the toilet, gulping in air, swallowing it down. Mateo's cum was the only flavor in my mouth.

I looked to where a mirror should be, above the sink, but it had been mysteriously missing when I was gifted this room to stay in.

My eyes moved to the bite marks on my wrists. Covering the scars that were left behind.

I shuddered, acutely aware of my nakedness, but for some reason, it wasn't bothering me as it normally did.

I settled on the toilet, doing my business.

I may be an emotional wreck, but that didn't mean I wanted to get a freaking UTI when all was said and done.

Flushing the toilet, I stepped into the now hot shower.

Only a moment later, Kazi opened the bathroom and joined me inside.

The scene caused a sense of déjà vu to roll down my spine. "I can't get James out of my mind," I admitted to Kazi watching his face carefully. It wasn't fair how I felt, but I also wanted him to know.

He smiled wistfully down at me. "I wouldn't have pegged him as your type."

I lifted an eyebrow.

"Mateo showed me James' pictures and if he's Izzy's dad, then well..." He tutted. "He's a bit... older?" Kazi reached behind me, grabbing the shampoo and rubbing it in his hands before scrubbing it into my hair, his strong fingers digging therapeutically into my scalp.

I closed my eyes letting out an appreciative groan. "You and Mateo are older too, you're in your mid-thirties, in case you haven't forgotten. And Mateo... wait how old is he anyways?"

Kazi snorted. "He's thirty-eight." His fingers paused. "Miss Yara, it's time. You need to tell me who your stalker is. I know you know. You've been keeping secrets."

I stiffened and forced myself to calm down. "That's rich."

Kazi, noticing my tension, began massaging me again before gently pushing me under the water to rinse my hair out. "Please?" The word was barely audible over the shower's spray.

My heart pounded uncomfortably in my chest, but he was right. He needed to know–this *stalker* wasn't going away. Clearly. "Young love can be an idiotic thing. Stupid. Naive. You walk into a relationship with a heart that has never been broken. Innocent, willing to do anything to make the other person happy. It takes a while to realize the difference between love and abuse when you haven't ever seen the difference. And some people get lucky, their love is pure, *true*. They find their person and they never have to experience that heartache." I shivered in the steaming water, leaning forward and finally opening my eyes.

I found Kazi's and used them for support. Strength.

"I wasn't that person. I didn't find love. I found a man looking for a pretty object. A precious angel." I spit the words out angrily. But the rage was directed towards myself, for falling into his trap. "My senior year of high school, I fell into a relationship with a coworker at the restaurant I worked at. He was older, the manager there. I was finally healing from the scars of my childhood."

I watched Kazi's face; he was one of the few people that knew that I was adopted, but I had never gone into the details of why. That story would be for a different day. His lips flattened in a tight line and I offered him a soft smile as the water from the shower dripped into my eyes, down my cheeks, to the ground below. It was reminiscent of tears; except I couldn't remember the last time I had shed any real ones.

"I ignored his advances for a while, but then he switched gears. He started to ask me about my day, my life. He seemed genuinely interested, like he was really trying to get to know me. Where I liked to hang out after school, my favorite hobbies, my friends. Except he was just trying to get as much information as he could to use it to get even closer to me."

Kazi grabbed the soap, and I was appreciative of the distraction as he lathered my body with it. The rough pads of his fingers skirting across my sensitive skin.

"Finally, after months, I gave in and went on a date with him." I stared at a stain on the shower's tile wall. "I'd like to say he forced himself on me the first time." The shape was reminiscent of a heart. I reached out, smudging it into something unrecognizable. Kazi's hands made their way to my waist and stayed there. A comforting warmth. "But that would be a lie, sure he pushed me a bit, but at the end of it I said yes. And in his car, after that first date, is where I lost my virginity."

I let out a dark laugh that was buried in the depths of my pain.

"How can you exactly explain the shame of agreeing to something you didn't want? That when you are pushed and pushed, you finally give in because it's easier than not to? How when you do give in, you realize the mistake that it was? That the man calls you a whore for it?"

"*Jagiya*." Kazi placed his head on my shoulder, his arms wrapping around me in a sturdy embrace. Even naked in the shower like this, I didn't feel uncomfortable.

"After taking my virginity, he decided he wouldn't stop there. He pressured me into a relationship. It wasn't long before we were practically living together—he was in his twenties and had his own place that I would stay at more often than not—and at that point? I wasn't sure how to escape. I was naïve, I didn't realize I could say no. That if I was in a relationship it didn't mean I owed him my body whenever he wanted it. I wanted to ask my adopted parents for help, ask Izzy, but I didn't want to be a burden. I was the idiot that fell into the trap, I needed to get myself out of it."

"You were a child," Kazi growled out.

I was shocked by the anger that flooded his tone, he was always the one that stayed calm, no matter what.

"I was eighteen." I snorted sardonically.

"He's right, you were a fucking child. Who the fuck is this *pendejo*?" Mateo's voice had me jerking my head in his direction.

He leaned against the bathroom door, fully naked, arms crossed over a broad chest.

I cast him a displeased look before turning back to the stain on the tile. It was a shapeless blob now.

"His name is Daniel. And he's partially the reason I started this company, why I changed my last name, and who has been sending the letters. I was hoping he would give up, that he could lose interest, but it seems he's the same asshole I met all those years ago."

Darkest Desires formed in my head as I lived in embarrassment of losing my virginity. Why should anyone live in shame for their wants and needs? Trapped in the nuances of polite society. Maybe if I had known that having fivesomes while wrapped in rope and covered in honey was perfectly okay, I would have realized I could have just left Daniel after the first encounter. That there was nothing wrong with what I did. I didn't need to stay with him just for the sake of the opinion of others.

I turned the water off, wiggling out of Kazi's arms. I cast a glance over to Mateo. "Rain check on my ass? I think I need a nap."

He didn't respond for a moment, and I turned around to see that he was now furiously typing on a phone. I had zero idea where he pulled that from, considering he was still naked.

Kazi gently guided me out of the shower, wrapping me in a towel.

Mateo finally looked up, his face cast in sinister shadows, except it didn't give me the heebie-jeebies. In fact, I found it oddly *sexy*.

Yeah, time to get on that medication as the therapist suggested.

"Sure thing, little bee, but I will be the first cock in that ass."

"So, you did hear me?" I laughed, knocking into him with my shoulder.

He caught me by the wrist, tugging me to him, and wrapping me in his large arms. "You know that I will kill anyone that deigns to hurt you? That I am the villain in this story?"

"There you go saying cheesy one-liners again." I crooked my neck to look him in the eyes. "I get the feeling you didn't talk a lot before we met."

Pain flickered through his eyes, his lips curling in a soft smile. "You'd be right. I hadn't found anyone worth the words. I guess I'll have to learn some new ones to impress you."

My heart swelled, and my eyes heated in emotion. "Let's all cuddle?" I asked the question, hesitantly, in a soft whisper.

Mateo smiled down, pressing a surprisingly soft kiss to my forehead. "Whatever you wish, little bee, but you're going to be squeezed into the middle."

Maybe even with the darkness that surrounded Mateo, the mystery that encapsulated Kazi, I would be okay.

Maybe they would be exactly what I needed.

Except James was still knocking at the back of my brain.

I would need to confront what had happened at some point, of our unreal connection.

But not yet.

Chapter 30

J.W.

James tapped his chair, looking down at his phone.

Why is she ignoring me? It seemed to go perfectly well?

He wracked his brain, trying to find the moment that everything went awry with Yara.

But he couldn't. Their chemistry had been unreal, but maybe that was the point.

She sold him a fantasy and he had fallen for it hook, line, and sinker.

Well, if she didn't want him, he would accept that. But he needed to have a conversation with her first. He needed closure. He rubbed a fist across his chest as anxiety and grief burrowed into his heart.

He couldn't have another woman he cared about disappear from his life without a trace.

He hadn't hurt like this since his daughter was taken from him in the dead of night. James did everything he could to find her, but it became clear that her *mother* had covered their tracks. He had sunk so much money into his search that his company had fallen to near bankruptcy. He would have lost it, too, if it weren't for–

"Knock, knock."

James looked up from his phone. Speaking of...

"Steve? What are you doing here?" James was surprised to see his partner in person. They had only met on a few occasions, conducting most of their business through phone calls and emails.

"You going to go on another discretion package with the CEO?" Steve walked into the office, shutting the door behind him and leaning against it.

There was something just a bit *off* with his tone, but James couldn't pinpoint it. And he wouldn't be questioning it, either.

Steve sought him out when he was at his lowest, offered him the funds needed to get his feet under him again.

James shifted uncomfortably in his seat. He had originally lied about why he was meeting Yara, he decided it best to follow through on the lie. "Yeah, couldn't find the right fit and we had a bit of an argument. I'm trying to get in touch with Yara to apologize and to find another match." The lie tasted bitter as it left him, but even more so?

James couldn't deny it, Steve had a weird interest in this entire encounter.

James hadn't thought much of it before, too wrapped in his own anxieties, but now he watched Steve with careful eyes.

"Hmm, Yara? She reminds me of a doll, except she needs to be put together a bit better."

"Doll?" The word caused sharp pangs of anxiety to hit him directly in the temple.

And the familiar tone Steve spoke in.

Did Steve *know* Yara?

Steve stepped further into the office, shadows following him until he stopped right in front of James's desk. Directly on the other side.

The lamp on it lit up his face eerily and shone directly on his bright cerulean eyes.

"Yes, a doll." Steve smiled, his face warping into the typical mask of emotionlessness that James was accustomed to. "Best to meet back up with her again. Let me know how it goes, will you?"

Steve reached forward and it took everything for James to not flinch back, but Steve just grabbed the frame from his desk. It was a picture of James's little girl on his shoulders.

"Isobella was so pretty here, so sad you lost her all those years ago. I wonder where she is now?" On those ominous words, Steve set the frame down, spun on his heel and left the office, shutting the door behind him.

It took James a few minutes to calm his nerves, and even longer to realize something.

He had never told Steve his daughter's name.

Chapter 31

MATEO

The maddening pitch of a phone woke Mateo from the best sleep he had ever had in his life.

He glanced down at the beautiful woman that was draped half-way across his body.

"Help me," he directed the words to Kazi. "Only you two and Emilio have this number."

The latter didn't say anything; he simply assisted with shifting Yara off Mateo.

Finally reaching the phone, he answered the call. "Boss."

"That's fucking rich since you sent me off like your errand boy."

"Information?" Mateo shifted on the bed, casting a glance back at Yara, she was still soundly asleep. His hand reached up on its own accord, brushing a piece of hair that had fallen across her face.

"I looked into the man, *James*, and into all of his business associates. She said his silent partner sent him to the company? Well here is where it gets weird, for all accounts and purposes, the silent partner is a complete ghost. I couldn't find anything on him. Except—" he paused.

"I told you not to tell him about James!" Kazi mouthed the words in anger at Mateo, but he brushed them off.

"Except what?" Mateo rumbled out.

"A home address. It is the only one listed on all the documentation I went through. Mateo, I don't know exactly what's going on, but you can't let anything happen to Yara, I'm too close to reuniting with Izzy. This would ruin it. I'm sending you the address now."

The phone disconnected.

A moment later, the address came through.

Mateo swore quietly into the room. He turned the phone's screen to Kazi. "Recognize this address?"

Mateo watched as the shock flashed across Kazi's face, his eyebrows knitting together, his skin draining of all its color.

"That's in the same building as our apartment. It's the floor above us," Kazi whispered the obvious into the space, tightening his hold on Yara who still slept soundly in his embrace. "What's going on? How does any of this make sense? If it's the stalker, why wouldn't they send the threatening letters there, if they knew where she lived?"

"Only one way to find out." Mateo stood carefully, stretching his body as he went and cracking his neck.

He bent down, ignoring Kazi, and placed a kiss on Yara's forehead before getting dressed.

He cast one wistful glance back at his little bee before leaving the room.

He needed to track down their only lead before it went cold, but he would be back. She wouldn't have to wait for him for long.

Chapter 32

YARA

"Mmmmm!" I stretched my arms out expecting contact on both sides, but only my left arm hit flesh.

"*Jagiya*," Kazi grumbled sleepily.

There he went with that word again, I really needed to search what it meant exactly. "Where is Mateo?" I asked a bit anxiously, he was noticeably missing from the bed. He wouldn't just disappear now, would he?

Kazi sat up, casting a cursory look around. "He'll be back. I'm sure he is doing something that you shouldn't worry yourself about."

What time is it?

I could barely see him, the room was enveloped in darkness still, but that didn't mean much with the shades drawn. Rolling over, I turned on a lamp and found my phone on the nightstand.

"Kazi, it's after 12:00PM! We need food." My stomach grumbled in agreement. I couldn't remember the last time I ate something and I was famished. "Go get me some, *please*?" I drawled out the word. "I'm craving shrimp."

"Really?" Kazi turned to me offering up a withering look. "Of course you are, well you are the boss. Fine, I'll be back." He leaned forward pressing a kiss to my lips. "I love you."

I covered my face in my pillow, embarrassment slithering across my skin. "Kazi, I don't think...I don't know..."

How does one explain that at twenty-eight years old they had never been in love before?

I wasn't even sure what it felt like. But there was one thing I was certain of. Kazi made me feel better than any other man in my life had.

But then what about Mateo... James... Why couldn't I help but think of them, too? Why was I so drawn to all three men in equal but inexplicably different ways?

"You don't have to say the words, I know you still need time to open up to this." His dark eyes simmered with heat. "But Yara? I'm okay with whomever you decide to bring into your bed as long as there is always space for me. I don't deserve you."

"Yara? No Miss? Did we just have to fuck to end that?" I giggled uneasily trying to make a joke to cover the confusing emotions that were crawling up my throat.

He let out a dramatic sigh. "I'll be back with food. Get dressed, let's go on a date?"

"Where's Mateo?" I asked again, watching Kazi as he stood up and got dressed. Covering his body. He was all lithe muscles. He was skinnier and smaller than Mateo and James, but he was no less attractive and my mouth went dry at the view.

"You gave the dog a bone." On that ominous note, he left the room.

I decided I didn't want to think too hard on that and decided it was going to be a lazy kind of day.

It was probably time to get up and do some work, but I deserved a vacation.

Turning the lamp off, I pulled the covers back over my head and quickly fell back asleep.

Chapter 33

YARA

It couldn't have been too much later that I heard a raspy, "Wake up, my precious angel."

Weight pressed down onto my chest, constricting my breathing; I spluttered in terror, unable to suck in air. Warm, wet, but sturdy shackles held me to the bed, trapping me in place. And through it all, the crippling darkness, the *dread*, of the unknown. Of what was to come next.

The feeling was one I was intimately familiar with–it crawled across my skin, burrowing deep into my gut.

This *wasn't* real. I was having a night terror, it *had* to be.

Years of terrible nightmares had taught me one thing, how to wake myself up.

Except no matter how much I tried to pull myself out of this one, I was still snared, unable to move.

This *wasn't* a nightmare, the realization caused me to finally blink my eyes open, my mouth opened to scream. Light flooded the room, I could see in my peripheral vision the window was broken, but my focus was drawn to the man that was imprisoning me.

"There's my angel. You kept away from me for so long, but I told you I would always find you. You are tied to me for life." Daniel's voice was vines that encircled me into the trauma of my past.

I was living in the present and in my memories synchronously.

Of when I had woken up to him just like this, except those times I hadn't remained calm. He enjoyed when I fought, loved to hear me scream, tried his best to make me cry.

"Get off of me." I glared up at him, his muddy eyes were glazed over, and for a moment, I wasn't even sure if he heard me.

"Yara, Yara, Yara. You aren't pretty enough to talk back, remember? Nobody likes ruined angels, but I took you in. A precious angel, scarred and flawed. I took pity on you. And then you ran from me." His monotone voice was more terrifying than if he was screaming into my face. "And now look at you. A filthy whore. Covered in not one but two men? I can smell them on you! You're covered in their marks. But they're both gone now, I watched them leave you. There's nobody here in this house except us." His eyes remained unfocused, I wasn't even sure if he was here in this moment, or if he was caught in the past. "How dare you?" He bit the words out, spit flying from his mouth landing on my face.

"I'm not yours. I am my own person." The words swirled into the tense room. I was doing my best to not lose my cool, to not let his voice alone unravel the years of progress I had made.

I held onto Mateo and Kazi, how they made me feel. I would make it out of this. They may not be here now, but they would return.

I knew I only had one chance. To scream. To fight. To escape this.

My heart pounded into my ears, I fisted the sheets below me.

He was using all of his body weight to push me into the mattress, his clammy moist hands encircling my wrists, his knees pinning my legs down.

The only part of my body that had any range of motion was my head.

What am I going to do?

He shifted, readjusting me and pulling my wrists above my head, one of his hands encapsulating them both. In his free hand, he now held a phone.

My missing phone.

A slideshow was playing. Pictures of me from that last month, through windows, from behind, across restaurants.

He had been vigilant.

He was talking *at* me still, but I ignored it, formulating a plan.

I wasn't the same teenage girl he put into a box so small that she had to reduce herself to fit.

Was I scared? *Terrified*.

But that wouldn't save me.

"You aren't even listening to me!" His enraged voice jolted me out of my calculations.

He threw the phone across the room, his now free hand finding the scar on my forehead. He stroked the puckered skin there.

It was the last mark he ever left on me.

It reignited my fire, this man wouldn't hurt me again. I wouldn't allow it. I could save my fucking self.

Reinvigorated and formulating a plan, I smiled softly at him. "I'm sorry that you couldn't get over me. I never stopped thinking about you either." The lie was bitter. I raised my head up, and he beamed at me, leaning down, incorrectly assuming I was going to kiss him.

Instead, my lips found his cheek and I opened my mouth. The smell of alcohol permeated my nostrils.

He let out a disgusting moan.

My teeth clamped down on his fleshy skin there.

He screamed; he hadn't expected it. He was caught so off guard that he let go of my wrists as he tried to yank back.

It was all I needed.

Tasting copper, I released my mouth from his bloodied cheek, spitting onto the bed.

In his discombobulated distress, I was able to push him back onto the mattress. With the newfound space between us, I attempted to jump away, but he caught me by the elbow, his fingers painfully pressing into my skin.

I began to scream, "Kazi! Mateo! Help!" Years of self-defense classes jumbled in my brain as a rage-fueled Daniel attempted to drag me onto him.

Fuck! No!

I fell back on him with all my body weight and heard a satisfying grunt as he let me go. With only a moment to spare, I used my legs and arms to roll over. We were close enough to the edge that by escaping his grasp, I tumbled to the ground.

The carpet burned my knees as I landed. It was the first time I realized I was entirely naked. Ignoring the disturbing realization, I got to my feet and searched the area for a weapon.

"Come here my precious angel, I just want to give you a fucking bite too." His tone was mocking as he got up, his face flushed, his cheek still bleeding. He appraised me, licking his lips. "Well you aged quite fucking well didn't you?" He zeroed in on the marks Mateo had left on my thighs. "But you're still a disgusting whore, aren't you?"

What am I supposed to do now?

I screamed for Kazi and Mateo. Tears attempted to escape my eyes, but I blinked them back fervently.

No, I can do this.

I leveled my gaze at Daniel. Instead of backing away, I took a step into his space.

He smiled smugly. "You always came crawling back to me, didn't you?"

I aimed for my next move.

He didn't expect my elbow to hit him directly in the throat.

Men never protect their throats. Izzy's voice reverberated around my mind.

He made a gurgling noise as he fell on his hands and knees.

I didn't wait. Didn't look back. I knew this would be my very last chance.

I bolted to the door and just as I tried to open it, it whipped open and knocked my hand into the wall.

"YARA!" the growl Mateo let out sent tingling waves of electricity all the way down to my toes.

I was safe. Everything was going to be okay. He spared me a quick glance before stomping into the room. Kazi was behind him, my lunch hanging from his hand.

"Get her out of here, and get her some fucking clothes," Mateo barked over his shoulder as he reached out, grabbing Daniel.

Kazi tried to tug on my wrist, but I dug my feet into the ground. "I'm not going anywhere," I argued.

Mateo looked at me as Daniel thrashed in his hold. If I wasn't staring directly into his eyes, I might have missed the moment they turned pitch black. "Suit yourself."

I watched in shock as Mateo secured Daniel's head in his bulky hands.

He moved so fast I almost didn't see him break his neck.

Almost didn't realize Daniel was dead.

Lifeless.

Almost didn't register the immediate *relief* I felt to know that my *stalker* was wiped away in less than a moment.

For a few moments we all stood in silence, a light breeze coming in through the broken window along with slivers of light.

"Thank you," I whispered the words before falling back into the comfort of Kazi's arms.

Using his strength as my own.

"Thank you?" Mateo dropped Daniel's corpse to the ground. "You're thanking me?" He took long strides until he stood directly in front of me.

Kazi set my food down. A jacket was wrapped around my shoulders. Kazi's arms encircled my waist from behind, his head going into the crook of my neck, his breath caressing my ear.

"You shouldn't be thanking me! I made a mistake! I followed the wrong trail. Yara, my little bee. We were almost too late." His hand reached up, fingers stroking along my mouth.

"I escaped him. I didn't need your help. I had it handled!" I was suddenly angry, outraged. How dare he?

"You did. You know he's dead don't you? You understand that I just killed him?"

I swallowed around the lump that formed in my throat. "I do."

"It's time we told her," Kazi murmured into my ear.

Mateo eyed me. "Yara, you're going back home for your reunion?"

I didn't bother to ask how he knew. "I..." I paused, I really didn't want to, but it was a month away, and I needed to talk to Izzy. "I am."

"That's where we will tell you all our secrets. Can you wait till then, mi pequeña abeja?"

I eyed Mateo, focused on Daniel, and then turned in Kazi's arms. "Kazi?" I asked, needing his reassurance.

I had noticed how he hadn't reacted to Mateo. How he almost seemed to know what was going to happen. "Yara, we'll tell you everything there. But please remember after all is said and done, I love you. And I have, for a very long time."

My heart beat painfully in my chest. Anxiety swirling with foreboding.

My eyes whipped to the broken window.

I thought I saw something move, but when I blinked, it was gone.

"Can I eat my shrimp now, please?" I asked, tugging out of Kazi's arms, reaching down for the bag, and leaving the room.

I paid no mind to Daniel.

Ignored the creeping unease that was racing through my veins.

Stamped down the dread of what I would learn of Mateo and Kazi.

Pushed away the memories of James.

I would deal with it all when I returned home, when I made it to the reunion.

Until then I would push my head into the sand and live in ignorant bliss.

I needed to, if only for myself, because otherwise?

I might have to admit that I was certifiable.

Chapter 34

D

*H*is doll.

D watched from the broken window as the man, Mateo, snapped Daniel's neck.

Mateo and Kazi, the two annoyances that had infiltrated her life. D surveyed the scene before him for a bit longer before deciding it was time to go.

Today wouldn't be the day for his doll to return to him. He would need to use James to lure Yara out.

James could be reunited with his daughter, Isobella.

And D could be reunited with his daughter, Yara.

EPILOGUE
One Month Later

It was the night of the reunion. A month had passed since the incident with Daniel. A busy month of catching up at work and not getting a moment to breathe until finally making it out here. To good old sunny Florida for my reunion.

Except I had still been too much of a scaredy cat to tell Izzy about her dad.

Except Kazi and Mateo hadn't revealed anything yet, but my guess was they were both in a gang or some equally nefarious lifestyle.

My stomach tossed uneasily, forcing me out of the bed I was currently sharing with Izzy in a hotel.

What the fuck?

I ran to the bathroom, upending my dinner from the night before and the small amount of wine I drank straight from the bottle.

Was the shrimp bad?

That's all I had eaten last night.

I settled a bit, and ignoring the mirror, I attempted to wash my mouth out.

What about the man that delivered my dinner? Why did he look so familiar?

He had a hat pulled over his eyes, but everything else was screaming that I knew him.

That would have to wait. I crawled back into bed with Izzy, careful not to jostle her. We had a reunion to go to, she had a man to fuck, and I had an entire traumatic event to unpack.

***

"Yara, get up!" Why was my dream shaking? Why was my stomach stabbing me in pain?

"Don't feel good," I garbled out. It was time to officially take shrimp off my menu; every time I ate them now, something bad happened.

Izzy sighed dramatically. "It was only one bottle of wine and we split it, you are not abandoning me for this."

Except it wasn't the wine, something else entirely was wrong with me. Something I had never felt before. This wasn't right.

I shot up as bile rose in my throat, running to the bathroom.

Barely making it to the toilet, I fell to the floor, retching loudly as I tried to empty the contents of my stomach, but there was nothing left to expel.

"You're not pregnant, are you?"

Pregnant?

The word jolted clarity through my mind.

Wait, when was the last time I had my period? So much had happened since my encounter with James, but it was before that. That was over a month ago.

I had gotten a birth control prescription right after I found out what Mateo had done to my implant.

And before that I had only fucked twice. James had a vasectomy. Kazi used a condom.

No, no, *no!*

"Shut up," I regurgitated the words out.

"You're not actually pregnant, are you?" Izzy began to stroke my back soothingly while holding my hair back for me.

I loved this fucking girl, but the thought made me sick. I gagged into the toilet below.

"Can I get you anything?" The concern in Izzy's voice was causing my guilt to sky-rocket.

"No." I needed to tell her about everything.

Daniel, Kazi, Mateo, James, and maybe one day, the trauma of my childhood. I was keeping so much of my life from her now.

Why was I even doing that? To protect her? To protect myself?

"You're not going to make it, are you?"

Fuck the fucking reunion. My stomach churned again, and I dry-heaved.

"I'm not. I can't be around those hellions in this condition. I woke up early this morning like this, but I was hoping it would go away." I tried to swallow down bitterness, hacking up the disgusting taste instead. "You are still going through with it. Both things."

She needed this and my own fuck-ups could wait.

"I have another room booked for you under an alias. There is a packet I want you to read and an NDA you need to sign. You need this." My body shook as I was forced to puke again, nothing coming out. Izzy needed this, she deserved this, to feel good.

She was finally going to do what she needed. Escape the vanilla men that flocked to her in waves. She was going to follow through on her darkest desires. And this man I had made sure to run the background check past Emil, I had met him in person, nothing would go wrong.

Izzy needed this. I could tell this breakup was hitting her harder than the last. Understandably so when your boyfriend fucks your god damn step-sister.

All of my misery and mistakes could wait. Including the strengthening possibility that I was *fucking* pregnant.

"Okay," she finally whispered out.

"Good. In my bag, the folder labeled *Come to Bed*," I yakked out.

My bestie was a freak in the best way. Somnophilia? Dormaphilia? She had me wanting to try a thing or two.

Izzy stopped her comforting, and I missed it immediately. "You know, you are going to catch these hands. How did you know what my plans were?"

If I wasn't dying, I would have laughed. "You forget, I am your best friend, and I know everything."

Best to not tell her I read through her entire profile when I said I wouldn't. Add it to my list of secrets.

"Now leave me to my misery. Nothing to do but wait till this passes. Throw me one of those fifty-dollar bottles of water from the mini bar first though, would you?" I would fake it till I make it.

"You've got jokes." I felt Izzy put my hair up for me, keeping it safe from the toxic waste below. "Feel better. You got your phone in case you need me?"

I finally removed my face from the toilet, lifting my phone and waving it at her. "You mean if you need *me*? If you bail on tonight, just know I will never let you live it down." I coughed and swallowed down another wave of bile creeping up my throat at the same time before leaning back over my unwanted home for the time being.

Izzy finally left me alone to my misery.

I could hear her talking to someone outside, but I ignored it.

I leaned back long enough to type out a text to Kazi, the more reasonable of my two men. I had banned them from coming near this floor, but I knew they were steaming on the one below.

> **Me:** *I cant stop puking. I neeeeed you to get me meds. Wait until Izzy leaves with Oliver and Maddox.*

> **Kazi:** *Okay, Miss Yara.*

> **Me:** *And I need you to bring me something else… PLEASE dont ask me about it.*

> **Kazi:** *What is it?!*

> **Me:** *A pregnancy test.*

I dropped my phone to the ground below, my forehead resting on the disgusting toilet lid. I ignored the incoming call. Kazi would do as I asked.

What if I am pregnant?

Which was more likely?

The condom failing, the birth control, or the vasectomy?

Fuck. I wasn't being serious about Izzy calling me mommy.

About the Author

So happy you made it this far!

I have one promise, every series I write will end in a HEA, but the path to it? Well, that will always be a bumpy ride.

Did you enjoy this book? If so, please check out my other works. I am also in the midst of quite a few other projects which you can check out on any of my social media platforms.

Want more in the Darkest Desires world? Check out Izzy's story in Come to Bed

Lastly, I have a Facebook group where I release information first: Sage's Sinners Dark Why Choose

Links to all of these can be found using this QR code.

-Sage

SNEAK PEEK

Here is a sneak peek at book one in my duet, Darkest Desires that follows Izzy.

Come to Bed

dorm·a·phil·i·a
a paraphilia characterized by sexual arousal or interest in engaging in sexual activities while asleep or unconscious

Prologue

Izzy did her best to calm her breathing and fall asleep. She found it difficult, because she knew when she woke up, it would be to a man. Inside her. Filling her up, fucking her, and fulfilling her darkest desire.

SAGE RELLEANNE
Dark
Why Choose
Romance
Come
to
Bed
DARKEST DESIRES BOOK 1